Where the Water Takes Us

Where
the
Water
Takes
Us

ALAN BARILLARO

CANDLEWICK PRESS

Copyright © 2023 by Nicolas Alan Barillaro
Epigraph from *Red: Passion and Patience in the Desert*
by Terry Tempest Williams, copyright © 2001, 2002 by Terry Tempest Williams.
Used by permission of Pantheon Books, an imprint of the Knopf Doubleday Publishing
Group, a division of Penguin Random House LLC. All rights reserved.

First edition 2023

Library of Congress Catalog Card Number 2022915354
ISBN 978-1-5362-2454-2

23 24 25 26 27 28 APS 10 9 8 7 6 5 4 3 2 1

Printed in Humen, Dongguan, China

This book was typeset in Adobe Garamond Pro.
The illustrations were done in watercolor and pencil and rendered digitally.

Candlewick Press
99 Dover Street
Somerville, Massachusetts 02144

www.candlewick.com

To Nancy

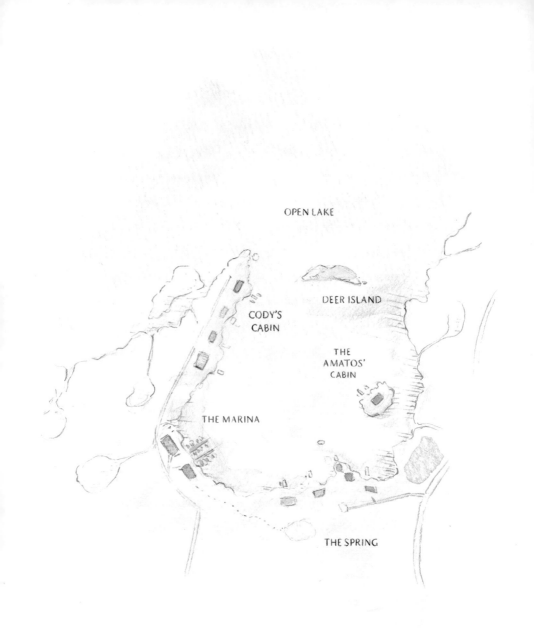

OPEN LAKE

DEER ISLAND

CODY'S
CABIN

THE
AMATOS'
CABIN

THE MARINA

THE SPRING

Wildness reminds us what it means to be human,
what we are connected to rather than
what we are separate from.

—*Terry Tempest Williams*

1

There are times when roads become rivers. Rivers with strong currents that pull you away and, whether you like it or not, take you far from home.

As her grandfather drove through the night, Ava couldn't help but feel that something horrible was going to happen to her mother. The thought never left her mind, even after the morning sun rose over the trees along the roadside.

The doctor said that her mother's pregnancy had become complicated, that from now on Ava would be more of a burden at home than a help. Ava still couldn't let go of the word. *Burden.* That's what the doctor had called her while she was sitting in the tiny office holding her mother's hand.

Her parents said otherwise. She could be as helpful as any eleven-year-old, but all the same, her grandfather arrived that weekend to take her to the lake. The far-off lake where her grandparents had a cabin on a remote island and where her father used to spend his summers. *Burden.* The word rang in her ears. From then on, Ava knew that all words were not equal. Some words had power. They had the power to change the entire direction of your life, if someone decided to say them aloud.

The road turned to gravel, and the lake appeared. "Here we are," Nonno said, pulling up to the empty marina. "You see? If we leave early enough, we still have the full day ahead of us." Her grandfather gathered all the groceries from town in his arms and carried them down to the docks. Morning mist still hung in the bay. Ava followed, the wheels of her suitcase leaving dew tracks behind her, until they came upon the familiar tin boat.

She sat at the bow, hugging her suitcase. "Did you miss coming to the lake?" Nonno asked as he started the outboard motor.

Ava nodded, but she wasn't thinking about that. She was only thinking about what she had just left behind. She'd been to her grandparents' place plenty of times, but this was the first time she'd ever been sent anywhere alone.

Nonno smiled as the marina shrank away. Ava couldn't tell if he was worried. She imagined that when you became an adult, you got better at hiding things. You learned how to get on with the day and climb in boats and no longer needed to bury your face behind your suitcase so that people didn't see you cry.

The engine whined as Nonno aimed the nose of the boat at the island cabin. "Look," Nonno called over the engine. He was squinting into the glittering sun, gesturing with his head toward the other side of the bay, with one hand on his hat to keep it from blowing away. "There's Nonna."

Ava's grandmother was standing at the edge of the dock with a blanket around her shoulders. Ava couldn't imagine how long her grandmother had been waiting for them to appear, but as the boat drifted closer, the one thing she could be sure of was that Nonna would know what to do about everything—everything unwanted that had come suddenly and without warning into Ava's life.

"Nonna!" Ava said, leaping from the boat to the dock. She hugged her grandmother tightly, not wanting to let go.

"Well, it's nice to see you too, bella," Nonna said, squeezing her back until the blanket wrapped them both. It was a hug worthy of Ava's faith in Nonna's ability to make everything better, and it told Ava that the terrible feeling inside of her, the one that warned her something horrible was about to happen, would soon pass. It was just a feeling, the hug told her. A feeling couldn't sweep her away.

2

"This is new," Nonna said, taking Ava's suitcase.

"My dad said I needed my own suitcase," Ava answered, staring at the dozens of dock spiders that had come out from the planks to escape the waves.

"Well, he's right," Nonna said, leading Ava up the dock. "It's your first trip alone. It's a big deal."

Ava followed Nonna up the steep incline of rock, through the dense garden that lined the shore. After three flights of stairs, they came to a sunlit porch full of hanging flowers and low baskets of herbs. Her grandparents' log cabin was perched at the highest point of the island

and overlooked the entire bay. Ava could even see the marina far off in the distance.

"Come on, let's get you settled," Nonna said, opening the front door. "No need for this blanket anymore! The sun's already getting warm."

"Mom packed some fresh tteok from the Korean market," Ava mumbled, hesitating to go inside. "I'm supposed to give it to you."

"Thank you," Nonna called from the hallway. "What we don't eat today, I'll put in the freezer."

At the doorway, there was a bucket filled with water. Ava tapped her foot against it, and the ripples of water vanished inside the bucket as quickly as they appeared.

"Nonna?" Ava said, still standing on the threshold.

"Yes, bella?" her grandmother answered.

"Is something bad going to happen to my mother?"

"Of course not," Nonna said, returning to the doorway. "Your mom is just having a baby. Two babies, in fact. Sometimes when you have twins, you need to take extra care is all. Didn't anyone explain this to you?"

"Maybe. But I wanted to ask *you*."

"Does your nonna look worried?" Nonna leaned into the sunlight. Ava looked anxiously into her grandmother's eyes, as green and gray as the island, and saw nothing in her expression that suggested she was lying.

"No," Ava finally replied.

Nonna put her hand to Ava's cheek, and Ava felt the roughness of her skin. "Remember, you're with your nonna. Now go change into your bathing suit. We'll have an early lunch outside while there aren't too many bugs out. I have to help Nonno bring up the groceries." She hurried down the steps. "Oh, and if you need to go number two, let Nonna know. You'll have to use that bucket. The power's out."

Ava looked down at the dirt-stained bucket of lake water and her stomach turned.

"I have to go to the bathroom in a bucket?"

"No, you silly goose," Nonna said from the steps below. "But we can't pump water from the lake without power. You'll have to pour that bucket in the toilet if it needs a flush."

"How are we going to do anything without power?"

"We can manage. Nonna knows lots of tricks. And maybe the power will be back in time for dinner."

Inside her father's old room, Ava found her suitcase standing next to the nightstand. It was where her family always stayed when they visited. The room was filled with familiar objects, reminding her how she was now alone. She grabbed the picture of her and her parents off the dresser and lay back on the bed, the family photo pressing against her chest. She closed her eyes, wishing she could go to sleep right then and wake up back in her own room, where the only thing she had to think about was when she was going to meet up with her best friend, Ruby Young, over summer break.

When Ava opened her eyes, the dark knots within the thick cabin logs were staring back at her in the shadows. How was it possible for her mother to stay in bed for over a month? Did the word *bedridden* really mean what she thought it meant? For instance, Ava couldn't figure out how her mother was supposed to go to the bathroom or put on her clothes if she wasn't allowed to get up. But these were only the first of Ava's questions.

The old-fashioned cream-colored phone sat on the

far nightstand. Her mother had said she wasn't allowed to have a cell phone until high school, so Ava would have to rely on the old landline. She picked it up to call her mother, but there was a trick to dialing out that she couldn't remember. More than once, Nonna had explained to her that the phone was on a party line, but Ava couldn't remember if that meant she had to dial the operator or the cabin number first. She only knew that sometimes other people would already be talking on the line when she picked up. She could just listen, and they wouldn't ever know. And sometimes when Nonna was talking to someone, a stranger would pick up and start dialing, and Nonna would have to explain that *she* was already on the line.

Ava put down the phone. She would have texted her mother from her computer, but the internet was another thing her grandparents didn't have. They'd have to drive to the library in town if Ava wanted to use it. Ava let out a moan. Nothing was easy at the cabin. Nothing was like home.

She changed into her favorite bathing suit, which she had rolled into a plastic bag and shoved into her suitcase when it was still damp. Putting on a wet bathing suit always made her need to go to the bathroom. She wondered if that made her strange, or if everyone had the same shivering urge. She only knew it was the truth— not that she'd ever dare tell anyone.

When Ava flicked on the bathroom light, the darkness remained, and she remembered about the power being out.

"No way," she said out loud, grabbing a swim towel. She ran outside with her shoes only half on, jumping past the bucket of water as she fled. "Not in a million years!"

3

The vegetable garden spread along the shorefront between the cabin steps and the main dock. Ava passed through the blossoming vegetables, unable to tell where one plant began and another ended. Everything seemed to stretch above her, reaching for the same sunlight that broke through the high pines. Vines twisted around the branches her grandfather had staked into the ground. The narrow clearing between the cabin steps and the shore was enough for a stone path and a small picnic table, yet even the picnic table carried clay pots that were overflowing with herbs.

"The water's very nice," her grandfather said. "You should jump in."

Ava leaned over the edge of the dock. Water striders and bugs too small for her to name moved on top of the water. Down below, rotten bits of leaves floated in and out of the light and tadpoles slithered in the shadows. A secret ugliness had suddenly shown itself.

"I like to go in slow," she said, pulling her swim towel around her shoulders. "And I like to see the bottom. In our pool you can see the bottom."

She waited for her grandfather to answer, but he was lost now within the sprawling vines. Her grandparents had lived on this island for so long, it seemed to Ava that they had taken on the same qualities as the island. The same wildness, she supposed, though she worried that wasn't the right way to describe it.

From somewhere within the greenery, her grandfather laughed. "Who needs a pool when we have a whole lake?"

Without warning, a loud boom echoed across the bay. Ava flinched. It sounded as if the entire cabin had all at once tumbled to the ground. The birds fled the tops of trees as a cloud of dust appeared.

"Nonno, what was that?"

Nonno leaned back out from behind the tall fava beans. "They're blasting to make way for the new road. It's been going on all summer. You'll get used to it."

Just then there was a rustling in the brush along the shore. A doe and her fawn appeared next to the dock. Ava didn't dare move or breathe as the doe slipped smoothly into the lake, leaving the fawn behind. The fawn bleated, calling to its mother and hesitant to enter the water, but the doe kept swimming.

Another blast erupted over the lake, this time scaring the fawn into the water. The small spotted deer swam right past the dock, next to Ava. She wanted to reach out and touch it but was too afraid.

"Where are they swimming to?" Ava whispered.

Nonno rested on his shovel and pointed out to the lake. "Oh, deer are always coming through. They're on the way to that island directly across from us. They call it Deer Island. That island's Crown land. No one can build on it, so those deer have the whole place to themselves."

Ava sat down on the dock, watching the fawn swim away. It was barely able to keep its head above water. It bobbed up and down so much that Ava worried it might drown. But it kept on going until it was reunited with its mother, and both began to graze under the white birch trees on the shoreline.

"That's amazing," Ava said, dropping her feet over the edge of the dock and kicking at the bugs until the water was clear around her. She felt the cool lake running through her toes. The sun was hot on her shoulders, and the urge to swim was irresistible.

She stood up, readying herself to jump in, her eyes still fixed on the deer. She drew a deep breath and broke into a run. As Ava leapt from the dock, she tucked her knees to her chest, all the while wondering if anyone, including Ruby, had seen something as amazing as a fawn swimming or even knew that deer could cross a lake. And just before she came splashing down into the water, she felt sure she had witnessed something extraordinary, something so special she might see it only once in her lifetime.

The lake water rushed in all around her, cooler and darker than her swimming pool but familiar enough that she couldn't help but enjoy it. Years of swim class had made her movements effortless, and as she came through the water in a forward crawl, she suddenly wanted to swim the entire day. She wondered if her grandfather might even let her swim out to the island to get another look at those deer.

After a while, a small cloud covered the sun and the entire bay fell into shadow. Ava flipped onto her back and looked up to fast-moving clouds, trying to be patient for the sun to return. She came across a cold spot in the water that made her shiver. Without the sun, the water was as dark as the pines around her. She looked back at the cabin and guilt overwhelmed her. Ava was having fun on the lake when her mother wasn't even able to leave her bed. Plus, there were those two babies kicking inside of her mother, who, Ava was sure, were causing all this trouble.

Ava swam back to the dock, determined to call home. She dried off, all the while looking back out onto the lake to see if the deer had disappeared. She thought about what her grandfather had said about those deer always swimming to the island and wondered if seeing that fawn wasn't so special after all. Maybe, Ava worried, Ruby would laugh at her if she ever dared to bring it up.

4

"Done so soon?" her grandfather called to her. He was standing under the slanting shoreline trees with a rope in his hand. "I was hoping you could help me tow those tomatoes back into the sun. That way I won't have to use the canoe." Her grandfather let the rope fall slack into the water. "Don't worry about this rope. I just tie it to the shore in case the anchor breaks. We don't want that dock to float away."

"Okay," Ava said, putting down her towel and slipping back into the lake. "I'll try." Ava swam over to the small dock overflowing with potted tomato plants. The dock was sitting just beyond the shoreline, covered in the shadow of a white cedar.

"Good. You just have to lift the anchor and swim the dock out into the sun. Tomatoes love the sun."

The anchor was only half a cinder block, tied to a thin yellow rope. It came up easily from the bottom, muddied and plastered with rotten leaves. Once the anchor was lifted, the small dock floated freely and was easy to hold on to and kick into the sun.

"Perfect," Nonno said, tying the extra rope to a tree. "Now see if you can pick a couple ripe ones for lunch."

Ava reached deep inside the tangle of velvety branches, searching the clusters of egg-shaped tomatoes until she came out with what she thought were the reddest ones. On the way back she swam one-handed, practicing her sidestroke.

"What a swimmer you are!" Nonna called, setting the picnic table. "You're like a fish!"

Ava smiled and handed her the tomatoes. "I just got certified for level ten. And I made the swim team again." She pulled herself out of the water and grabbed her towel.

"Is that so? Well, you know that means you're big enough to take the canoe out after lunch."

Ava stopped drying herself and looked down at the

green canoe tied to the side of the dock. "Without you?"

"Without me. We'll put something heavy at the front so you can paddle straight. You can go around the islands, but you still have to wear a life jacket. That's the deal."

"Okay." Ava hesitated. She knew she ought to be excited, never having had the chance to take out the canoe alone. But she couldn't seem to manage it. Another booming sound came from the road along the mainland and Ava jumped, but Nonna didn't even seem to notice it.

"Come and eat," Nonna said, calling her to the picnic table. "Here you go, bella." Her grandmother handed her a plate full of food.

"Maybe we can call my parents after lunch?" Ava said, picking at her greens. Something about being woken up so early made her stomach unsettled. She wasn't the least bit hungry.

"I already called to tell them you got in safe. They said to enjoy the lake and they'll talk to you tonight."

Ava looked back at the canoe. To her, tonight felt far away. She wondered why she was suddenly so afraid of things that only last summer she enjoyed. If her parents had been with her, she would have begged to take out the canoe.

She was just being a big chicken, she told herself. But she didn't know what to do about it. She put a piece of soft cheese in her mouth and forced it down. Ava imagined this must be the new her, like that time when a tooth came in double the size of the others, or when she found out her feet had grown so quickly she no longer fit into her favorite shoes. She'd just have to find a way to get used to it.

5

The cinder block landed in the front of the canoe with a hollow thud, lifting Ava in her seat like a seesaw. "It makes a good anchor too," Nonna joked, tossing a nylon rope inside as well. The many uses her grandparents had for concrete blocks amazed her: Blocks propped up the bottom of the stairs and held open doors. They bordered the garden and parts of the shoreline and anchored the corners of docks.

"Buon viaggio," Nonna said, shoving her off. Ava stiffened as the canoe shot out from the dock. "Just keep that life jacket on and stay in the bay. Stick along the shore if you get nervous."

"Okay." After a few strokes Ava steadied herself and found a rhythm to paddling that made the canoe more manageable. She set off toward the back side of her grandparents' island, where the distance to the mainland was shortest.

Once Ava had made the cross, she could see the construction of the new road through a clearing in the trees. She canoed past the dirt parking lot, filled with dump trucks, and in the distance saw an excavator hauling the blasted chunks of rocks and kicking up so much dust that it powdered the surrounding leaves white.

The farther Ava paddled, the more the road pulled away from the lake and disappeared into the dense pines. Along the base of the bay were dozens of cabins, hidden like mushrooms in the shadows of the trees, each with its dock along the water. The dock Ava liked best had a slide at the end, and there was a baby-blue boathouse next to it where an old woman was reading. The woman waved as Ava passed. Ava waved back, as she had seen her grandfather do many times whenever another boat came by—quietly, never saying a word.

The opposite end of the bay was much busier than her

grandparents' side of the lake. Larger boats were rushing in and out of the marina, some racing out to the open water. Each time one roared off, the waves rocked the canoe until Ava was convinced she would tip over.

Ava waited for a break between the boats. The first chance she got, she paddled quickly past the traffic of the marina. *Okay, calm down,* she told herself, clumsily turning back toward the shoreline. *Even if they tip you, it's not like you can't swim.*

Beyond the marina was a row of small cottages. There were no cars, and the windows were shuttered so that the places all seemed empty. All but the last. There, a shirtless boy stood on the dock holding a fishing rod. He held the rod high over his head, swinging it wildly back and forth. It struck Ava as strange, and she drifted closer to get a better look. Before Ava knew it, the boy broke into a run and whipped his fishing rod forward. He released the line, but the silvery lure didn't get anywhere near the water. Instead, the lure shot up in the air and got caught in branches of the pines that stood over the dock.

"Oh, come on," the boy groaned, straining to free his lure. He had a mess of brown hair and freckles, and

Ava was sure he couldn't have been much older than her. He leaned back on his rod and grunted. "I'm just a little stuck," he said with no embarrassment. "It's a new rod. I need to get the feel of it."

Ava didn't answer. There was something about the boy that told her she should keep away. He reminded her of certain boys at her school. The ones who talked too loudly and were always too excited about something. If you ever had to sit next to them in class, you'd see that by the end of the day, they'd be in some sort of trouble.

She decided to make a fast escape, but the canoe only leaned when Ava really needed it to turn. She panicked as she raced forward toward the shore and the boy. "Sorry!" she called, wincing as her canoe scraped the front of the boy's dock. She tried to paddle in reverse, horribly embarrassed, but the boy wasn't paying any attention. He was too busy battling the tree above as if there were some fantastic-sized fish within the branches, until the line fell onto the dock and the boy.

"I got it!" the boy cheered, brushing the fine pine needles from his lure. He jumped back when he noticed that Ava was right alongside him. "That's cool," he said, relaxing. "You can hang out and watch me fish. I don't mind the audience."

"I'm not hanging out with you," Ava exclaimed. "I'm just trying to turn." Ava grabbed ahold of the dock and desperately pushed herself free. "There," she said, taking up her paddle again.

"Wait, where are you going? You don't understand the bites I got today. I think there's pike in this lake. You ever seen a pike?"

"No," Ava answered, not caring what a pike even was.

"Well, you're going to want to see one, trust me. It's the ugliest fish you'd ever see in your life. They've been around since the dinosaurs."

"No thank you," Ava said, too embarrassed to even look back in the boy's direction. She was humiliated to think that he assumed she had meant to paddle up to his dock and have some sort of conversation.

"I'll catch one and then you'll see what I'm talking about!" he shouted to her. "Don't worry, I can show it to you on your way back."

"I won't be back," Ava said, paddling out beyond the safety of the shallows, leaving the shirtless boy behind.

The wind rushed in off the open lake, and the waves made a slapping sound against the hull of the canoe that unnerved her. Still, Ava decided it was better to cross the rougher waters at the center of the bay than to turn around and face the boy again. Besides that, right between where she was now and her grandparents' place was Deer Island.

The island looked completely different from the vantage point of the open lake. It had a crescent-shaped cove hidden from the rest of the bay. The cove was marked by fallen trees that poked out from the water, all of them branchless and gray. Ava supposed they all had fallen long ago.

Ava couldn't resist paddling into the cove, wanting to catch another glimpse of those deer. There, everything was surprisingly quiet and still. Shafts of sunlight broke through the canopy of birches and lit the bright green reeds. Buzzing in and out of the small pools of light were countless dragonflies and damselflies. They flew around her in every sparkling color, gleaning the dust-sized insects that filled the air in little swarming clouds. A slim dragonfly rested on the nose of the canoe. It was a powdered dancer, blue and bright.

"No wonder those deer come here," Ava whispered. She put down her paddle and let the canoe drift a little deeper into the emerald-colored reeds. The sign on the shore read CROWN LAND. NO TRESPASSING in bold red letters.

It was then that something tickled the top of her hand. Ava brought her hand to her face, and a large insect came into view: a brown comet darner, perched on her knuckle. It shot into the air buzzing so loudly and frantically that its wings brushed up against Ava's nose. Ava jerked backward as she tried to wave the massive dragonfly away. The canoe swung wildly to one side and tipped. Ava screamed.

The dragonflies and damselflies scattered as Ava pulled herself up out of the knee-deep muddy water. "Oh, come on," she groaned, wiping the long strands of algae from her face. It took all her strength to drag the upside-down canoe to shore. She opened her life jacket and let the mud and slime escape, spilling down her clothes.

The no trespassing sign loomed over her.

"Look, I'll go as soon as I can. It's not like I wanted to fall in," she muttered.

A gust of wind rippled the surface of the water and rustled the tops of the trees, leaving goosebumps on Ava's skin. Ava sat down and rinsed the mud from her ruined shoes. She looked back into the gray birches, hoping to catch a glimpse of the deer, but saw nothing besides the trees. She lay back on the rocks, exhausted. The day wasn't even close to being over, but it already seemed longer to Ava than any day she could remember. They had left for lake country in what felt like the middle of the night, and now her tiredness overtook her.

Closing her eyes, she waited for her energy to return. Somewhere in the trees a woodpecker continued knocking, keeping her from falling asleep. She took a breath and thought back to her life at home before twin brothers and frightening hospital visits. But the longer Ava held her eyes closed, the more it felt like her old life was disappearing, and if she opened her eyes, not only would that life be gone, but an entirely new life was sure to take its place.

6

Acorns fell from the bear oak trees in the wind, one after another plopping into the shallow cove. A light rain came down, and Ava blinked against the wind. She was still somewhere between sleep and realizing she was not in her bed.

Then a deep rumble of thunder jolted her awake. A wall of rain was heading toward her, rushing into the bay from the open lake. Ava scrambled to her feet, trying to gather her shoes, but the gale was so strong it sent them tumbling across the dirt. She grabbed hold of the canoe. "Come on!" she said, tugging but unable to flip it upright.

A bolt of lightning stretched across the sky, and before

Ava could move, the full power of the rain came all at once, hitting the cove so hard that she was sure it would devour everything in its path.

Ava wanted to run for the shelter of the inland trees, but the birches swayed wildly above her as the wind tried to tear them from their roots. She had no choice but to crawl underneath the overturned canoe. She pulled her legs against her chest and curled into a ball. *What do I do? What do I do?*

The storm came heavier, pounding like it would chip away at the island until nothing was left of it. Ava heard an awful crash when a tree toppled somewhere nearby. Its fallen branches came hard against the ground, scraping against the canoe until it tilted to one side and Ava was left half-exposed.

A flash of red feathers jumped out from the leaves, rustling at Ava's feet. The woodpecker thrashed about, its wings moving in ways that were unnatural and told Ava instantly that something was wrong.

Terrified, Ava brought the canoe back down around her and covered her ears. "I don't know how to help you! I'm sorry; I don't know what to do!"

When the wind and rain finally came to a stop, all that remained was the sound of the wet leaves, beaten and heavy with rain, dripping into the lake. Somewhere under the branches of the fallen tree, the woodpecker had quieted.

Ava rubbed the tears from her eyes, trying to convince herself that the silence meant the woodpecker was well enough to have flown away. She waited until the sun appeared and made the air under the canoe so stuffy and warm that she had no choice but to climb out.

Outside of the canoe, a single red feather was waiting. It blew around the dirt and settled gently at Ava's feet. Ava picked up the feather. And then, a few feet away, she found the dead woodpecker. Its head was angled, and its eyes were open as though it was still alive and nothing so terrible had happened. But something terrible did happen. The proof was there, staring back at her.

7

Ava leaned over the lifeless bird. She had never seen anything bigger than a bumble bee die in front of her, and contrary to what Ruby had told her, death didn't look like sleeping. Instead, Ava thought the woodpecker seemed strangely awake in how powerful its beak still appeared to her, and how the shafts of its bright red feathers still glistened in the sun. It looked as though at any moment the bird would turn and fly away.

"You okay there?" cried a voice, and for a moment Ava thought it was the woodpecker who had spoken. But then a fishing boat pulled into the cove, the kind that had several fishing rods and nets propped up along the side. At the front of the bow leaned the same shirtless boy from earlier in the day. "See!" he said, pointing at Ava. "I told you she was in trouble!"

"That was quite a storm," a man called to her, cutting the engine. "No one saw that coming. It was all over the radio." He walked to the back of the boat and tilted not one but two outboard motors from the water. "Cody here said we should come check on you. I guess he was right."

Cody smiled, puffing out his chest. *What was there to smile about, and why not put on some clothes?* Ava wanted to ask him, but she didn't dare say anything. Instead, she hid the red feather behind her back.

The reeds brushed against the hull of the big fishing boat as it coasted into the cove. "Cody, make sure I don't run us into the rocks. I'm still getting the hang of driving this thing."

Cody leapt into the water, rope in hand. He was squatting low and walked sideways as you'd expect a crab to walk, staring into the shallow water. "All clear, Dad!" he shouted. "Hey, do you think this is a good spot for fishing?"

The hull made an awful scraping sound against the rocks, and everybody flinched. Cody looked sheepishly at his father. Ava saw her chance to escape.

"Well, I'm going now," Ava said, finding her shoes. "The island's all yours."

"Wow!" Cody cried. He pulled back the branches that lay atop the canoe. "You did a number on this thing, didn't you! Dad, how can we tow her? The hull is probably cracked. It'll spring a leak!"

"No, it's not," Ava argued, feeling the deep scratches along the hull of the canoe. The paint was chipped, but there were no cracks that Ava could see.

"Hey," Cody said, turning his attention to Ava. "What do you have in your hands?"

"Nothing," Ava replied, slipping the red feather into her pocket. The boy had so many freckles on his face that she thought it made him look unwashed. Ava glanced at her feet, afraid of what he might find. What if he thought she was responsible for everything bad that had just happened?

Ava looked around for the woodpecker, but the bird was hidden by the fallen branches.

"What's the big deal?" Cody said. "Why can't I see what you got?"

"Cody MacDonald, mind your own p's and q's and get back here," the man said, climbing out of the boat. He took off his hat, and Ava saw clearly how his thick mustache and equally thick eyebrows seemed to hold in a permanently sad expression. He lifted one end of the canoe up, testing the weight of it.

"Never been in a canoe myself," he said, looking up to the sky. "Wouldn't trust them if one of those storms came through again. Not without a motor at least. We can help you out just in case the weather turns . . . We're the MacDonalds by the way—"

"Not like the restaurant," Cody interrupted. "Our name has got an *a* in it."

"We're renting the place around the corner for the summer," Mr. MacDonald went on. "Rented this boat too, from the marina right in this bay. We're on a fishing trip of sorts. We're kind of celebrating our time together." He looked at Cody and smiled. "Anyway," he said, turning back to Ava. "I'm betting we'll be neighbors. Is that right?"

"I guess," Ava answered, not wanting to accept she'd be in lake country that long.

"Well, how about we be good neighbors then and get you home safely, just in case that storm shows up again? Sound like a fair deal?"

Ava glanced up at the dark, fast-moving clouds.

"I'm sure your parents are worried about where you are," Mr. MacDonald added. "I'd feel bad if we didn't help."

Ava wondered if what Mr. MacDonald said was true, and whether her parents were even thinking about her at all. How could they? They were spending all their worrying elsewhere. But after Mr. MacDonald had put the thought into her head, Ava did remember her grandparents and was concerned they might be driving around in their boat looking for her.

"Do you know the island behind this one?" Ava asked.

"I think so," Mr. MacDonald answered. "The marina told us the best fishing is over there. What was that name they kept saying? Something Italian."

"Amato," Cody jumped in. "That's the name they said."

"Is that right?" Mr. MacDonald asked Ava.

"Yes, that's it," Ava admitted. It was a strange thing, Ava thought, that the MacDonalds knew about her grandparents before she knew a thing about the MacDonalds, that people at a marina would be talking about your family when you didn't even know it. It somehow made Ava feel better about lake country, less lonely.

She stepped forward to get a closer look at the MacDonalds' boat. It was clearly the faster way back to her grandparents' cabin, and she'd be grateful to leave the dead woodpecker behind. As far as Ava was concerned, the sooner she could forget that Deer Island ever existed, the better.

"Well, aren't you going to tell us your name?" Cody said, rubbing his head.

"It's Ava," she replied, so anxious to get going that she started to lift one end of the canoe. "Ava Amato."

8

The lake was flat, reflecting the pink afternoon sky, when Mr. MacDonald's boat arrived in front of Ava's grand-parents' island, the canoe lying across the back.

"I still can't believe that's your place," Cody MacDonald shouted, his voice carrying across the bay. "There's got to be tons of fish around here! Look how deep the water is!"

"Ava, are you all right?" Nonna said from the dock. "Nonno is off looking for you. We couldn't see you in the bay."

"I was on Deer Island," Ava explained, "and a tree fell on the canoe!" Mr. MacDonald's boat lurched backward as he struggled to park it alongside the dock. Ava stumbled back in her seat while the boat rocked. "But the canoe's fine," she continued, hopping off the moment she could manage it. "It just got all scratched. I could have paddled home, I swear, but the MacDonalds said it was safer to give me a ride."

"Close enough," Mr. MacDonald said, stopping the engine.

Cody rushed to the side of the boat and put out his hand. "I'm Cody," he announced proudly to Nonna. "Cody MacDonald."

"Nice to meet you," Nonna said, taking his hand, but instead of shaking it, she used it to pull Cody and Mr. MacDonald's boat smoothly against the dock.

"Thank you," Mr. MacDonald said. He went to the back of his boat and slid the canoe into the water. "We weren't sure this could get her home if another storm came in," he explained. He handed Cody the rope for the canoe. "Cody, please bring it around the other side of the dock and tie it down."

Cody gladly hopped onto Ava's dock, dragging the canoe behind him.

"I got it," Ava said, taking the rope from him.

Cody shrugged and turned his attention to Nonna. "I saw the whole thing," he said, pointing at Ava. "She was in some serious danger, but luckily I was there to help."

"I wasn't in danger," Ava complained. "I don't even need that canoe. For your information, I could swim across this bay right now if I wanted to."

Cody covered his mouth and laughed. "Swim the whole bay? No way."

Ava wanted to argue with him, but she couldn't say in front of her grandmother what she wanted to say to Cody MacDonald right then.

"It was a bad storm," Nonna said, getting between them. "I haven't seen one move in that quickly in twenty years."

Mr. MacDonald bent down to study the controls before putting the boat into reverse.

"Well, we better get going," he said. "I'm sure we'll see you again, Ava. We're around all summer, just on the other side of the bay."

"Then we'll have to have you both over for dinner one night," Nonna said brightly. "Won't we, Ava?"

Ava winced at the thought, refusing to answer, not that her opinion seemed to matter. Cody MacDonald had leapt onto his boat and was grinning back at Nonna, clearly thrilled by the idea.

"That's very kind of you, thanks," Mr. MacDonald said, steering the boat clear of the dock. "See, Cody? Our vacation is already off to a great start. Another cause for celebration."

For Ava, the idea of having some strange boy over for dinner sounded absolutely horrible. She promised herself that later she would convince Nonna not to go through with it. Unlike the MacDonalds, she wasn't here to have fun. She was here for a terrible reason. Her grandparents would understand that. There was no point to having the MacDonalds for dinner. Ava couldn't be surer of it.

9

By nightfall the power had returned, and water could be pumped in from the lake. Ava took a warm shower and changed into her pajamas. Her dirty clothes were in a heap on the floor. The red feather lay on the sink. Ava wondered if she was strange for keeping the feather. It was a memory of something horrible, but at the same time she couldn't help but be fascinated by it. Maybe keeping it made her weird, but maybe she had always been weird and just didn't know it until right then.

Steam poured out of the bathroom when Ava opened the door. She found Nonno patiently repositioning the television antenna, making the reception flicker in and out at various levels of fuzziness. Ava didn't say a thing about it, knowing from past conversations that Nonno would want to explain to her all about the Canadian Shield. For reasons Ava never understood, the rock surrounding them interfered with the reception of her parents' cell phones and prevented the internet and phone service from working as they should.

"There, now doesn't that feel better?" Nonna said from the kitchen. "It's nice to have our hot water and power back."

Ava smiled, her cheeks flushed and the red feather now tucked in one hand. Nonna had been busy making dinner. A pillow-sized piece of dough stretched across the counter. Steam was rising from all four pots on the stove, and empty baking sheets lay on the counter, sprinkled with flour.

"Want to help?" Nonna said, holding up a knitting needle. Never in her life had Ava remembered her grandmother speaking to her without being in the middle of doing something.

"Maybe next time," Ava answered quietly.

Nonna swiftly cut the dough into small pieces. She laid the needle over a single piece of dough, rolling it quickly back and forth until the dough stretched the full length of the needle and a pasta noodle had magically formed. Ava looked at the feather in her hand.

"Nonna?"

"Yes, bella," Nonna said, her attention focused on the dough.

"What would you do if you saw an animal get really hurt? Are you supposed to try and help it?"

"Well, that depends on what kind of animal it was, I guess, and if I could help it. Maybe not a hungry bear or a moose!" Nonna laughed.

A handful of flour hit the counter and again the rolling continued.

"What if it was a small animal? Something smaller than me . . . like a bird?"

"Well, some birds bring good luck if you help them, but either way, yes, you should help it." Her grandmother's hands picked up speed. "Do you remember the barn swallows that nested over our back door last spring, those ones that kept pooping all over my nice doormat?"

Ava nodded.

"Do you remember when you came to visit how I wouldn't let your grandfather knock down that nest? That's because a bird nesting over your door is said to bring good luck."

"Good luck?"

"Yes, good luck, but you have to be careful not to let them fly into the house."

"Why can't they fly into the house?"

Nonna glanced up at her and laughed. "When I was a little girl," she said, rolling the dough faster and faster, "the old spinsters used to say that a bird in the house brings a death into the family. I don't believe it now, of course. But back then I was scared stiff that I might let it happen. I had to sleep with my sister whenever I thought about it. It's the same if a bird falls from the sky dead or dies at your doorstep. It's like a curse being put on you. It's a sign that a death will come to the family."

"A death!" The word rang in Ava's ears.

Nonna's smile dropped when she saw the deep fear in her granddaughter's face.

"Oh, but those are only stories."

"But you just said . . ." Ava thought of her mother and choked on her words. "You said there's going to be a death in the family."

"Nothing bad is going to happen, and no one is going to die," Nonna answered, dropping what she was doing. "Your Nonna is silly for telling you such stories. I was just trying to make you laugh. There are enough things in the world to worry about. Don't start worrying about silly curses. Here . . . taste the sauce."

She took Ava to the stove. Nonna's glasses fogged as she leaned over the many pots. She came back with a wooden spoon full of tomato sauce and held it in front of Ava. Ava looked up at her grandmother as she reached for the spoon, trying to believe with all her heart that there was no such thing as a curse.

The sauce was warm and smooth against her lips.

"Good?" Nonna said, knowing there was only one answer, as this sauce was Ava's favorite.

"Yes." And Ava surrendered, the sweetness of the tomatoes still on her tongue.

Nonna's smile returned. The wooden spoon swung in her hands like the wand of a fairy godmother and landed gently on the tip of Ava's nose, leaving a dab of sauce behind.

"Good," she said. She dumped a full tray of pasta into the boiling water. The water bubbled and hissed. "Then go sit down. Dinner is just about ready."

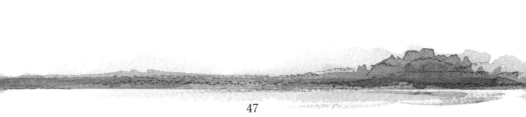

10

In the darkness, Ava dreamt.

A woodpecker flapped in the moonlight. Its feathers were silver, and it brought its heavy beak to a tree and pecked until there was an awful drumming against the hollow wood . . .

The water came up from the soil. It rose above her ankles . . .

Above her waist . . .

Surrounding her, until the current pulled at her clothes . . .

The woodpecker flashed its wings and cried out, but the more it cried, the more it sounded to Ava like laughter.

When Ava awoke, her heart was racing. She felt the wetness of her sheets around her thighs. Her pajamas were soaked as she climbed out of the bed. The cedar floor creaked and was cold against her bare feet. She entered her grandparents' room and went to Nonna's side of the bed. "Nonna," Ava said softly, touching her grandmother's shoulder.

"Yes, bella," Nonna mumbled, her eyes still closed.

"I'm sorry. I had an accident."

Nonna rubbed Ava's back. "Nothing to be sorry for," Nonna said, half asleep.

Still, as Ava made her way to the bathroom, she couldn't help but feel ashamed. *What eleven-year-old still wets her bed?* she thought. Her doctor had told her it was more common than she thought and that she'd grow out of it eventually. But no one Ava's age ever talked about it, and Ava certainly wasn't going to admit it. So she never had any way of knowing if what the doctor had said was true.

Ava changed into clean pajamas while her grandmother switched out the sheets. Back in bed, Ava listened to the wind blowing outside, knocking the trees against one another with a hollow sound that, to Ava, didn't sound like trees at all. *They found me,* she thought, listening to all that knocking in the darkness.

She imagined a flock of woodpeckers gathering outside her window. "She's the one," they were saying. No matter how hard Ava tried to ignore them, the woodpeckers kept on. It was the same as wetting her bed. A terrible secret that she wished would go away remained.

"I'm sorry," Ava finally said, though what could an apology mean to woodpeckers, she wondered. But they knew exactly what she had done. They had come for her.

11

"Sent to the hospital," Nonna said, cradling the phone. "For how long? I see . . . That sounds serious, Arlo. Do you need us to come there?"

Ava stood in the doorway with a swim towel around her shoulders. There was no mistaking the worry in her grandmother's voice.

"Of course, Ava is fine with us. Just call us back as soon as you hear the results of the test. Hold on, Arlo. You should tell Ava yourself . . . Ava, come to the phone. Your father has something important to tell you."

Ava couldn't bring herself to walk inside. Instead, she clutched the feather that was hidden in her palm. She woke that morning believing that the feather might hold some sort of unknown power, like an amulet that could protect or hurt her, though until that moment she wasn't sure which. She squeezed the feather tighter, and the quill poked sharply against her skin.

"Ava, come here, please. It's about your mother."

Ava shook her head and stuffed the feather in the pocket of the shorts that she wore over her bathing suit. Whatever her father was going to tell her right then, Ava didn't want to hear it. She let the screen door slam behind her and took off down the cabin steps.

"Ava!" Nonna called after her, but Ava was already on the dock and untying the scratched-up canoe. She pushed off from the island, but her paddling was all wrong, and she had forgotten the cinder block. "Come on," she said, straining as the front end of the canoe kept out of the water, veering to the side each time her paddle struck the surface. No matter what Ava tried, there was no steadying the canoe.

It's like a curse being put on you, she remembered Nonna saying. *It's a sign that a death will come to the family.*

"A death in the family," Ava repeated, her eyes filling with tears. "Mom, I'm sorry."

She was unsure whether she believed in curses, but what she believed was real or imagined had nothing to do with it. All Ava knew for sure was that her mother was in the hospital, and saving her mother was all that mattered to her. Whether she liked it or not, she had to go back to Deer Island and that woodpecker.

12

Ava stood over the pile of feathers and bones, all that remained of the woodpecker after just one night. "Look, I'm sorry that you died, I really am, but that's no reason to hurt my mother. You can't take her. Do you hear me? You can't."

Ava kneeled over the dead bird, staring at it until the silence made her hands tremble. She wiped her wet cheeks, trying to calm herself. "There was nothing I could do to save you . . . Do you understand that? What could I do? Tell me what I was supposed to do."

The cove kept silent. Not even those working the marina could be heard within the shelter of birch trees.

Ava brushed away the ants crawling around the bones. She dug her fingers into the sandy dirt and began to make a hole. She pulled small stones from the lake—the prettiest Ava could find—and one after the other stacked them until they were in a neat pile. Finally, she took the red feather from the canoe and carefully pinned it within the stones until the feather stood upright. The afternoon sun made everything uncomfortably warm.

"Okay. There. Is that better?" she said, backing away. "Look, if you're going to curse me, at least let me know, okay? Give me a sign." Ava looked around the cove, waiting for some sort of answer, but the cove was still.

"Fine. I'll pick something." Ava got in her canoe and pushed off into the reeds. "If I'm cursed, make a fish jump or a rainbow appear, or a cat fall from the sky. Something, okay? I don't care what. I'll count to five, but you can't start until I say."

Ava placed her paddle across her legs and closed her eyes.

"Okay, I'm ready . . . One. Two. Three. Four . . . Five."

The moment she finished counting, a large fish

jumped clear out of the water, landing behind her with a distinct *plop*.

Ava swung around to see the unmistakable rings rippling toward her. "No!" she cried, lunging clumsily to the other end of the canoe to plead with the feather. "That doesn't count. You're too late. I already counted to five." But Ava couldn't be sure how the rules of a curse worked exactly.

"Look, there's got to be some other way." She couldn't bring herself to admit what she truly was thinking. She was frightened to say it out loud.

She looked around the cove, suddenly worried that someone was there watching her. She cupped her hands around her mouth, not wanting even the deer to hear what she was about to say, not the trees or the dragonflies or the ants that devour small things whole in the night.

"We could make a deal that we don't tell anyone about," Ava whispered. "It would be like a trade . . . You just can't take her, okay? You can take *them* if you have to, but you gotta leave her out of it."

Ava sat back in the canoe but couldn't find the strength to paddle. "Okay," she said, exhausted. "At the count of five. Do we have a deal? One. Two . . . Three . . ."

At first, the wind came into the cove as an uncertain breeze. The tops of the trees shimmered in the sun, loosening the acorns from the bear oaks, until the gust grew strong enough that a number of the heaviest acorns fell, splashing into water. A frog leapt for the safety of the lake, scattering the dragonflies and damselflies away.

Ava's eyes went wide. "It's a deal then," she said, picking up her paddle. She pushed off from the cove, with a strange sort of calm she'd never known. She didn't feel relief but resolve. The deal was made. She was sure of it, just as she was sure that there was no turning back from the thing she had said.

She paddled steadily home. Though her nerves were on edge, it was clear to Ava what she needed to do next. She needed to hear her mother's voice on the phone, assuring her that everything was okay. No matter how horrible the curse would be, and no matter what became of her brothers, her mother would be left out of it. That was the deal.

13

"Nonna! Nonna!" Ava called, running as fast as she could up the stone path. "You have to help me with the phone. I have to call my mom and dad, and I don't know how to do that party line thingy!"

Nonna was halfway up the stairs. Freshly picked carrots and herbs were spilling out over her arms. "Don't 'Nonna' me," she said, stopping. "If you're so big to run off, you don't need my help for anything. And you should listen more when I explain something for the first time."

"But mom's better now. I know it. Can I just call to make sure?"

"They're still at the hospital, Ava. I'm sorry, but we

just have to wait for their call. And I'm sure they're fine. We have to get used to this. Having twins can be complicated, and the doctors are only trying to be extra safe, not just for the babies but for your mother. It's a good thing they're being extra careful. Do you understand?"

Ava slumped onto the stairs. "But what am I supposed to do until they call?"

"Write her a letter."

"A letter?"

"Yes. Everyone loves to get a letter. Write your parents a letter and go down to the marina and mail it."

Ava sighed. "I'd rather just call."

"Keeping busy will cure your nerves, believe me," Nonna said, walking up to the cabin. "And after you're done at the marina, you can head to the spring. That spring water is better than anything you can get from a tap or the lake, and we're almost out."

Ava stood up and moaned.

"And see if Nonno wants to go with you. He'll show you where the empty jugs are. You two are cut from the same cloth. You both need the distraction."

Ava came down the steps and looked around. "Nonno?" she said half-heartedly, not really wanting to find him and go to the spring. She squatted down along the stone path and instantly recognized two pots overflowing with heart-shaped leaves. Her mother had put together the pots for her grandparents, and Ava remembered picking out the color of the pots and helping add the soil. They were sweet potatoes, and it was the stems of the sweet potato that her mother always made and that were Ava's absolute favorite banchan. "I just want to go home," she said to the pot.

"Ava?" Nonno said, appearing from the garden. "Is that you?"

"It's me," Ava answered.

"Good," he said, holding a bucket full of weeds. "Did you talk to Nonna? Please don't be too worried about your mother. Things are going to be fine."

Ava kept on brushing her hand across the tops of the sweet potato leaves, not saying anything at all. Nonno flipped the bucket over and sat down. For a moment he was silent. "Did I ever tell you about the time your dad let a bear into the house?"

Ava looked up, surprised. "No, definitely not."

"One summer he got it in his head that he should make friends with the squirrels."

"Squirrels?"

"Yes, but what he didn't tell us was he was leaving all sorts of food on the windowsill to try and feed them. We woke up one night with your dad screaming 'Bear! Bear! Bear!'"

"A bear can swim to the island?" Ava asked.

"Of course. And I ran into your father's room and found a big black bear coming right through the window."

"What did you do?"

"Nothing. Can you believe it? I looked into that bear's eyes, and I was shaking. I thought to myself, I can't stop this bear from coming in this house."

Ava waited for her grandfather to continue, but he just sat there looking back at her. "Wait," Ava said. "But what happened?"

"Nothing. That was it." Nonno clapped and then whistled. "Like that, the bear was gone. Your dad thought I was very brave standing up to that bear. I had to tell him I was just plain scared. What do you think? Was it okay that your nonno was scared of that bear?"

"I think so," Ava said.

"Bravo." Nonno laughed, standing up. "And one other thing. You should know your mother and father just want you to enjoy the summer. That's all. They're not trying to keep you away up here. You shouldn't be mad at them."

Ava sighed. "Nonna said I should write a letter and mail it at the marina. She wants you and me to go to the spring."

"Why not? What else do we have to do?" Nonno started off down to the dock. "You go write your letter and I'll get the jugs and the boat ready. A walk to the spring is just what we need. Believe me."

14

It was so hot, Ava and her grandfather barely spoke as they followed the steep gravel road that wound up into the hills behind the marina. The higher they climbed, the more Ava noticed the last bit of coolness from the lake disappear and the full heat of the day pressing down on her.

Halfway up the hill, Ava put down her jugs and swatted the mosquitoes away. She couldn't understand why the mosquitoes were so much fonder of her than they were of her grandfather. She would have asked him, but she heard something a little ways behind them in the brush. Ava turned around, hoping it was a fawn. But instead, Cody MacDonald appeared from the thimbleberry

bushes, licking his fingers. He carried with him a small empty jug of his own.

"Isn't that the boy Nonna said you're friends with?" Nonno said.

"Friends with him?" Ava grimaced. "No way."

"Going to the spring too?" Cody shouted, announcing himself.

"Nothing special about that," Ava mumbled, trying to get her grandfather to walk faster, but the more she tried to rush, the more he seemed to take his time. "Everyone goes to this spring."

"That's what I heard," Cody said, running up alongside Ava. "So I had to try it. And did you notice how soft your hair gets from the water around here? What's in this lake?" Cody leaned the top of his head toward Ava. "Feel how soft my hair is. Go ahead. Feel it. It's so weird!"

"No thanks," Ava said, shoving Cody away.

The hill leveled out and around them was a flat, sun-filled clearing. Nonno hunched down next to a sloping bit of rock. The rock was black and damp, and there was a simple spout coming out of it where spring water flowed. "Here we are," Nonno said. "Do you remember this place?"

Ava shook her head. She was surprised to see how small the spring was. She had imagined a large stream, but instead the water bubbled up from somewhere under the earth, hidden by all the moss and ferns around it. Ava could have walked past a million times without ever noticing it.

"Well, the last time you came up here you were very young." Nonno smiled. He cupped his hands under the spout and smelled the water. "The lake water is safe if you have the right filters, but nothing beats the water from this spring." He took a drink. "It's nice and cold. That means the water is still good. If the spring is running slow, the summer heat will spoil it."

Nonno added water to the first jug, swished it around, and dumped it.

"That's good to know," Cody said, squatting down next to him. He had a stick in his hand and was whipping the tops of the tall grass clean off. "My dad says if I like this place so much, we'll come back next summer. He's letting me choose. Maybe I should pick a bigger lake though. It would be nice to try renting a speedboat."

Nonno took a handkerchief from his pocket, wiped

his forehead, and smiled politely at Cody. "Do you think you two city kids can carry these jugs home by yourselves? I'm going to keep on. I'd like to get a longer walk in. The doctor said at my age it's good to walk."

"For sure!" Cody said to Ava's horror. He tossed his stick aside and stood next to Ava.

"What?" Ava said, stepping farther away from Cody. "But how will you get home if I take the canoe?"

Nonno took an old branch from the grass and examined it. "Oh, someone from the marina will give me a ride, if you can manage the canoe." He stepped on the branch until it cracked and all that was left was a straight walking stick, which he waved at them. "See you back home, Ava."

Ava's face flushed as Nonno disappeared into the woods. She was unable to look over at Cody MacDonald. It was the second time in two days she was stuck talking to him. She hoped by some miracle he would just go away.

"I'll fill my jug first, since it looks like I'll be doing all the work anyway." Cody moved her water jugs aside.

"No way!" Ava argued, tipping his jug over. "And I never asked you to help me."

"Like you can lift four jugs of water out of here on your own," he said, and laughed at her. "By the way, you can't keep expecting me to save you every time you need help. I'm not your babysitter."

"It's you that needs the babysitter. Why are you always following me around? It's creepy. How did you even know about this spring?"

Cody righted his jug under the spout and raised his chin. "Fishermen talk, that's why. They told me down at the marina. And you're not the only one on this lake that likes spring water, you know. The world doesn't revolve around you, Ava Amato."

"Don't you think I know that?" Ava said sharply. She walked off, wanting to be as far away from Cody MacDonald as humanly possible. She plopped herself in the grass and faced the lake, her back squarely turned to him. She kept arguing with Cody in her mind, frustrated she hadn't thought of something better to say back to him. What did he know about what she was going through? Ava doubted Cody's mother was in the hospital or that anyone in his family had something as awful as a curse on their head.

She pulled at the grass and looked out at the lake and its endless maze of islands, inlets, and bays, waiting for Cody to leave so she'd never have to see or speak to him again. But Cody didn't leave, and Ava felt he was being as annoying as possible, taking his time, washing the outside of his jug, and whistling just to bother her.

Ava tried her best not to pay attention to anything he was doing. From the hilltop she could see the marina below, where the cottagers were going about their normal day and looked as small as toy figurines. Being up that high looking down at the lake made her feel far from everyone she loved. Ava felt Nonna was wrong about going to the spring. It didn't calm her nerves or help one bit.

The distant red tin roof of her grandparents' cabin reflected in the sunlight. "I shouldn't be here," Ava said quietly to herself. "I should be anywhere but here."

She made the mistake of checking to see if Cody was finished filling his jug, and he smiled back at her as if they were best friends. "Enjoying some alone time?" he said, slapping at a mosquito that had landed on the back of his neck. "That's cool. I get it."

"Anywhere but here," Ava repeated.

"What's did you say?" Cody asked. "You're mumbling."

Ava glared at Cody. "Nothing."

15

"Your turn," Cody said, still squatting over the spring. He was drinking directly from the spout, and the water was splashing all over him. Ava swore she saw his lips against the spout as he drank, like he was kissing the thing. He looked back at Ava, water dripping down from his mouth onto his shirtless chest. "What?" he said, wiping his mouth with the full length of his arm.

"You're gross, that's what," Ava answered, not even knowing where to begin. Ava walked back through the high grass, nearly stepping on two blue stones. They were speckled brown and poking out of the grass.

"No way," Ava gasped, dropping to her knees. They weren't stones at all. She gently scooped the two eggs in her hands and brought them closer. She trembled when she realized they were warm and she was holding something that was not just fragile but alive.

"Hey!" Cody said, rushing over. "Those are robin's eggs. You can't just take them!" He started searching the grass until he came back with two solid clumps of a nest. "Look! It's a broken nest! What if their mother's still around? They could have just fallen from a tree or something."

Ava wanted to argue with him, to tell him to mind his own business, but he'd put the idea in her head that there was a mother robin somewhere in the trees looking for her eggs and there was no ignoring it. Cody swiped the eggs from her hands.

"Hey!" Ava protested, but she was unable to resist him, fearing the eggs would break.

"Relax," he answered, placing the eggs in the nest. He walked over to a small sugar maple and reached up onto his tiptoes, carefully placing the broken nest with the two eggs in the crook of the tree. "Okay," he said, running back to her. He took Ava's hand and yanked her down with him into the grass.

"Now we hide right here," he said softly. "We have to wait and see if the mother is coming back."

Ava lay quietly, not daring to breathe, Cody's hand still holding onto hers. It was the first time a boy had held her hand. It wasn't something Ava had ever wanted to happen or cared about, but she noticed it all the same, just as she noticed the smell of the dry grass and felt the hot sun that made her forehead damp with sweat.

Whether she had wanted to or not, she now knew exactly what it felt like to hold Cody MacDonald's hand. He had hands that were slender and warm. Hands that seemed a little longer and bonier than hers and that were sticky with sweat.

She was thankful that his eyes were still locked on the nest and so he didn't see her embarrassment. She freed her hand and pinned it under her elbow. There was a long and unbearable silence where nothing happened, but Ava didn't say a word. She was waiting to see what he would do, but he kept still, not moving a muscle.

Ava saw a genuine look of concern in his eyes, and for

the first time, she wondered if Cody MacDonald could be trusted. "It's a sign," she whispered.

"A sign of what?"

Ava looked hard at him, still unable to decide if she could tell him things that she hadn't told anyone else, not even her grandmother. The way she was staring at him seemed to make him shift in the grass. "Do you believe someone can be cursed?" she asked.

"Sure," he said. "Why? You cursed or something?"

"I don't know. Maybe . . . Yes. I'm for sure cursed."

He nodded, not saying anything for a moment. All the concentration drained from his face. "That adds up, actually. You act kind of weird most of the time."

Ava wanted to argue, but he wasn't wrong. Lately, she didn't exactly feel like herself. And so the two of them sat there in silence, listening and looking for the mother. They heard the muffled sound of the spring spilling onto the rocks, overflowing into the moss and ferns, while the four jugs shone in the sun. Little white butterflies and small bugs danced in the thick summer air, but nothing was biting at them.

"Is this enough time?" Ava whispered. "I don't think she's coming back."

"We should wait a bit longer, just in case."

"Well, in the meantime, can I ask you something?"

"Sure."

"Don't take it the wrong way, but why don't you wear a shirt? It's kind of strange, don't you think?"

Cody looked at himself and, as though for the very first time noticing his nakedness, he blushed. "It's—it's the summer," he stammered. "I never wear a shirt in the summer." He scratched at his shoulder blades, looking uncomfortable, and Ava wondered if a bug had just bitten him.

He could no longer keep still and had to stand up from his spot. "I guess the mom's not coming," he said, covering his bare chest with his arms. "I bet you that storm knocked that nest down. I should take the eggs with me. You don't know anything about raising baby birds."

"And you do?" Ava said, leaping up. "Besides, how do you know that I don't?"

"I did a project once on robins."

Ava raced toward the tree. "Whatever! I need it! I'm the one who's cursed, remember?" Ava cradled the broken nest in her arms, and before Cody could stop her, she was off, running down the narrow path of the hill.

"Hey!" he called after her. "What about your water? And what do those birds have to do with you being cursed?"

"I'll tell you later!" Ava shouted, disappearing down the path. "Leave the water. I'll come back for it!"

"Leave it?" Cody said, looking around at all the jugs. There were more water jugs than hands.

He brushed off the blades of grass from his bare skin. "It's the summer," he mumbled, staring at his chest. He stood there a good while before he tried to carry all the water jugs at once. After a dozen or so tries, he found a way, complaining to himself as he struggled back down the path.

16

"Nonna! Nonna!" Ava screamed, pressing her face against the screen door. Ava's hair was full of leaves and her face muddy as if she had taken the whole forest along with her. "Nonna!"

"What happened?" Nonna said, rushing over.

Ava backed away from the door. "I found two eggs. Can I bring them into the house to show you, or is it bad luck?"

"Now don't start that again," Nonna said. She pushed her glasses up the bridge of her nose. "I wish I had never brought up that curse business. These are robin's eggs. Where did you find them?"

"Up by the spring!" Ava's feet couldn't stay in one place. She leaned close to the eggs. "Robins? Really?"

"Yes, robins. Where's Nonno? Where's the water?"

"He went for a walk in the woods. I found the eggs, and I waited for the mother, but there wasn't one, I promise. You can ask Cody. He was there. Please, can I keep them?"

Nonna tossed the dish towel over her shoulder and gave a look that worried Ava. It was the look that said, "No way will this ever happen." Ava's heart sank.

"People aren't allowed to take care of wild birds, Ava. There's a law against it. You need a permit. And it's a lot of work to raise one, never mind two."

"But you used to volunteer at the shelter. They let you do it before. You've told me so. We can't just let them die and do nothing!"

"Ava, their shells are probably too cold and cracked." Nonna took a tissue from her pocket and leaned down to examine the eggs more closely. She turned them gently, one after the other. Ava saw her grandmother's eyes soften.

Nonna sighed. "Leave them here with me. We don't need to be shaking them around. You go get a pot from the shed. Nothing too big. These eggs have to be kept warm."

"Thank you, Nonna!" Ava shouted, running down the cabin steps as fast as her legs could take her. She couldn't help but believe that raising two robins would mean something against the curse. She was protecting the lives of these two birds and her mother.

At the bottom of the stairs, Ava forgot entirely where she was going and ran for a moment in the wrong direction. "The shed!" she shouted, leaping between the plants—trying to find a shortcut out of the garden without stepping on anything. "I have to go to the shed!"

17

The lake was quiet that afternoon. Not a single motor-boat came into the bay, and the cabin was humid and warm except when a north breeze blew in through the kitchen window and made a hushing sound through the trees. Ava and her grandmother had cleared the coffee table and moved it to the corner. Ava hovered over it, looking into the makeshift nest made from an old terra-cotta pot and filled halfway with a cut-up towel. There was a lamp that Nonna had clamped to the pot and turned on to keep the eggs warm.

"Your father called, you know," Nonna said quietly, reaching out to feel the temperature of the light. "They're observing your mother for the night, but he wants you to know that everything's fine, and they'll be home from the hospital tomorrow. It was just a real scare. The doctors are keeping a close eye on her, so no need for us to worry. Anyway, he told me to tell you that he misses you, and they will call again tonight. Okay?"

Ava looked at the two eggs, beaming. "I knew it," she whispered into the pot.

"Knew what?" Nonna asked, getting up. "And tell me, now, how much time do we have until we turn them?"

Ava squinted at the clock. "Four hours," she said, ignoring Nonna's first question.

"That's right. Good girl. Mark them with a pencil so we know which side is which while I get a soup going."

"Nonna?"

"Yes?" Nonna said, turning on the stove.

"If I take care of these two birds, that'd be really good luck, right?"

"It would be a very kind thing to do, yes. But luck doesn't have anything to do with it. It's difficult work to raise robins—and a lot of responsibility. They're going to rely on you, Ava, like you're their mother. When they hatch, you'll have to feed them every twenty minutes."

"Every *twenty minutes?*"

"Until they're fledglings, anyway. And at least we don't have to feed them after sunset. Don't worry, I'll check in on them at night. Old people are up at all hours, anyway, but young ladies need their sleep. But remember, they are *your* responsibility."

"Okay, got it."

"Good. Now wash your hands so you can help me get dinner going."

There was a knock at the screen door. Nonna leaned out the kitchen window. "Who could that be?" she said to Ava, taking care to first shut off the stove. "When you live on an island, you don't expect many visitors."

Nonna stepped onto the porch. At her feet were four filled water jugs, shining brightly in the sun. She put her hands to her hips. Somewhere, beyond the cabin view, the soft hum of a motorboat faded across the bay.

18

Ava lay back on the dock in her swimsuit, staring up at the white sky. The morning was cool and overcast, but Ava already had the sense that the clouds wouldn't last. Soon the afternoon sun would be blazing, leaving the air sticky and thick.

Last night, Nonna had held a bright light up to each egg so that, for a fleeting second, Ava could see through the shell. It was like when you pressed against a flashlight and saw right through your finger in a sort of reddish glow. Ava was disappointed that instead of seeing a baby bird, she saw what looked like a big spider trapped inside the shell. But Nonna said this was a good sign and told her that in a week the two eggs would hatch.

One week, Ava thought. She could just about make it, if she kept patient.

"Morning!" Cody MacDonald shouted from the water, startling her. Ava sat up to see him pulling up in a small aluminum runabout with a sparkly red stripe down the side.

"Hey," Ava said. "You've got to come in and meet Hazel and Red. Wait until you get a look at them."

"Look yourself!" Cody beamed, opening his arms. "Meet the Beast! My dad just got it for me at the marina. My very own boat! Can you believe it?"

"You called it the Beast?" Ava frowned.

"Of course! A boat's gotta have a cool name. I'm going to take it out of the bay. You want to come?"

Ava hesitated. His boat had the smallest outboard motor Ava had ever seen. More than that, he somehow looked different to her. It was then that she realized that Cody MacDonald was wearing a T-shirt.

"Are you even old enough to drive it?" she asked.

Cody patted the engine. "It's way under ten horsepower, so that's a yes. Hop in!"

"I can't. I'm supposed to look after Hazel and Red."

"Who? You mean those robin's eggs? They haven't even hatched yet. Come on, we won't be gone long. Besides, I found a place that has plenty of worms. And you'll need a whole pile of worms for two birds."

Ava looked at him. "Can't we just buy worms at the marina? I don't want to dig anything up."

"Fresh is better, trust me. Look, I swear I'll get you the grossest monster worms you've ever seen. Grab a can or something to carry them in."

Ava flinched at the thought. Cody put one foot up on the gunwale of his boat, as if acting like the captain of a pirate ship. "Look. I gotta set sail. Do you want to take care of them or not?"

Ava imagined Hazel and Red staring up at her from the pot, flapping their wings and hungry. "All right, all right. Just wait here."

She ran off inside to ask Nonna, who was quick to agree.

"Cody!" Nonna shouted from the screen porch, the surprise of which sent him off-balance and the boat teetering. "You stay clear of the open lake. Keep that boat of yours close to shore. And make sure you both wear a life jacket. You understand me?"

"Sure thing, Mrs. Amato!" he yelled back. Cody reached under the seat of his boat and pulled out two bright orange life jackets. "See," he said, waving them. "We're all set!"

"Thanks, Nonna! I promise I won't be long!" Ava called. She turned to Cody, panicked. "Oh no. I forgot a can."

"No problem," he said, straining to click the last buckle of his life jacket. "We can use my tackle box. I'll just empty it." He sat back down and started the engine.

"All right!" he shouted over the revving throttle. "Prepare for the power of the Beast!" The tiny four-horsepower outboard gurgled into gear, rocking gently from side to side before laboring to roll forward. "And we're off!" The boat fell into a slow crawl.

Ava hung her arm over the side of the boat, feeling the water glide through her fingers. "Can't it go any faster?" she asked.

"What do you mean? There's two of us weighing it down. This is fast!"

Ava couldn't help but laugh. His ridiculousness was

somehow growing on her. It's not that she always liked the weird things he did, but he somehow made her feel less strange about herself. That was how Cody MacDonald made her feel, she suddenly realized. *Less strange.*

19

"It must be too hot today," Cody complained, the front half of him deep within a hole he had dug in the dirt. "I can only find mealworms." They had traveled to a small strip of beach that Cody had made her swear not to tell anyone about. Cody placed yet another beetle larva inside his tackle box and, crouching on all fours, kept on digging. Under the shade of the dense pines, the ground was dark and moist.

"Wouldn't it be better if you had a shovel?" Ava asked.

"You don't get it, do you? You've got to *feel* for them with your hands. That's how you find the big ones."

Ava picked at the upturned dirt with a twig. There

was one giant earthworm trying to find its way back underground. She watched it for a moment without saying a word, wondering how a worm knew up from down, especially after its world had just been turned upside-down by Cody MacDonald.

"Wow," Cody said, coming up from his hole. He pushed Ava by her shoulder. "Look at the size of that one! Didn't I tell you this was the spot?"

The giant worm wrapped itself around the twig until it coiled into a thick knot. It was as alive as Hazel and Red, or Cody MacDonald, or her. Ava frowned. She didn't feel she had the right to take that worm from the ground and do what they were meaning to do with it.

"Doesn't it seem kind of cruel?" she asked.

"What do you mean?"

"I mean, we're killing one thing just so another thing can live."

Cody squinted at Ava and then the worm. "They're just worms," he finally answered, and returned to his hole, digging.

"Well, can't baby robins eat something else?"

"Maybe bugs. Like ants or something."

"I mean, anything that's not living and breathing."

"I think they eat berries too. But they definitely need worms to live."

"What do I have to do?" Ava said, staring at the worm pulsating around the twig.

"I think you have to mash them up with an ax or something."

"I don't think so," Ava said, putting the giant worm into the tackle box. She wanted to forget the whole business of mashing worms and get back to the cabin to check on Hazel and Red. She walked down to the lake to wash her hands, but no matter how much she scrubbed, they wouldn't come clean.

"Grab some sand and use it like soap," he said, carefully closing his tackle box full of mealworms. He was caked from head to toe in dirt, and the dirt fell from his hair as he walked back to the boat. "Don't you know that's the only way to keep clean? I learned that in summer camp. Didn't your parents ever send you to camp?"

"No," Ava said. She took a clump of sand and began to scrub. She slipped into the deeper water, unable to resist swimming out into the sun. "My grandmother says it will be about three weeks before Hazel and Red can really fly," she said, scrubbing her knees. "So I just have to make it three more weeks. That's it. After that, everything will be back to normal. I think by then my curse should be lifted."

"You keep mentioning that curse, like I'm supposed to know what you're talking about."

"It's probably better that you don't know anything about it. All that matters is that I keep my promise. Everything will work out if Hazel and Red stay healthy."

"What if they don't stay healthy? Are you triple cursed?"

Ava's stomach turned. "Why would you even say that? My mother just got out of the hospital, Cody."

"Sorry," he said softly. "I didn't mean to joke about it." He leaned on the Beast, resting his head along the gunwale. "Anyway, in three weeks, summer will be over. I'll be heading home. My dad will make me pull the Beast out of the water. I guess we'll have to find a place to tarp it for the winter. No boat, no more freedom."

He reached out his muddy hand to touch the sparkly

red stripe of the Beast. For a moment, Ava wondered if he was going to burst into tears.

"Well, I *want* to go home," she said.

"Home's fine, I guess." He sighed. "I got two homes now. My parents got divorced this year. Anyway, I got this sweet fishing trip and a boat out of the deal because my dad feels so bad about it, so I guess I shouldn't complain. Are your parents together?"

Ava nodded, not sure what to say.

"That's good," Cody said. He looked up at Ava, and in that moment, Ava saw a side of Cody she'd never seen. He took a deep breath, and his chest sank like a tire deflating.

Ava smiled back at him, unsure how to make him feel better.

"Honestly," Cody told her, "I don't even know what home means anymore. All I know is I don't ever want to say bye to the Beast. I mean it. I hope these next three weeks last forever."

20

The cabin was cold and dark as the sun had yet to lift above the trees. "Nonna!" Ava screamed, pulling on her grandmother's hand. "Come, quick!"

"Okay, quiet down," Nonna said, getting out of bed. "They'll hear you across the lake."

Ava led Nonna to the nest. Inside the pot lay a baby robin. Its yellow bottom poked out from the broken bits of shell. There wasn't a single feather on the little bird, only a tuft of fuzz along the back and head.

"It's naked!" Ava said.

"Of course it's naked." Nonna laughed. "It's a baby."

The hatchling struggled upright. Its eyes were closed, and its feet were big and shaking.

"This egg must have been laid first. The second one should hatch tomorrow, then. Which one is this?"

"That's Hazel. She's got more brown on the bottom of her egg. See? Right there."

"Well, it's nice to meet you, Hazel. I'm not sure if you're a boy or a girl, but what does it matter? You look well enough. First things first. Let's get you warm." Nonna came back from the closet with another clamp light and attached it to a small orange crate. "Wash your hands and grab a clean towel. It's time to get started."

That morning, Nonna didn't ask Ava what she wanted for breakfast or to get dressed. She was too busy readying the crate and making Hazel food and telling Ava all that needed to be done to be sure that Hazel was properly taken care of.

Ava sat by Hazel's side, following each instruction, all the while staring down at the naked bird glowing under the warm lamplight. Hazel's skin was nearly see-through, and her dark round eyes looked to Ava as if they were sewn shut. Ava wanted Hazel to be beautiful, but Hazel didn't look beautiful at all. She looked ugly and helpless.

Ava got so anxious inspecting the little bird that she bumped the crate by mistake, and instead of Hazel tumbling over, her head reached up and her mouth sprang open as wide as a fish's. "Look at that," Nonna said. "It can't see us, but it felt you bumping against the crate. It thinks you're its mother returning to the nest. That's a good sign that it's hungry."

Nonna placed a syringe gently into Hazel's mouth. "We'll have to feed it every twenty minutes from now on," she said, putting the watery mix of minced worms at the back of Hazel's tongue. "Just a little at a time, like this. Make sure they swallow it all. They're like little children. Always hungry. They'll ask for food even when their mouths are full. Don't worry, I'll keep track of the amount of food and water and their weight until you get the hang of it."

Ava nodded. The more Nonna explained the routine of the day, the more Ava grew concerned. She kept a close eye on Hazel's slightest movements for any sign of something wrong. There were dangers everywhere: a slight change of temperature or a small mistake in how much

95

water Hazel was given or a single missed meal. All this, Nonna told her, might mean something very serious for the little bird.

It wasn't until Nonna forced Ava to wash up for lunch that she got up from the floor and left Hazel's side. She had yet to brush her teeth or change out of her pajamas. That all seemed unimportant to her now. Ava's day was being reshaped by Hazel, rearranged around twenty-minute intervals of when Hazel needed to be fed.

By the next morning, Red was born too, and there were two birds to care for and keep track of. Although Ava didn't want to show that she was exhausted, there was no hiding it from her grandmother. "Go sit on the dock and rest in the sun," Nonna said to her, but Ava shook her head sharply and refused. She needed to prove that she was able to help. That she wasn't a burden.

As the day went along, time blurred, the minutes and hours mashed together just like the bits of worm and bugs that Ava was taught to make into bird food. Hazel and Red opened their beaks, crying for the syringes that Ava had prepared, forever reaching, gaping from sunrise to sunset, demanding all they could from her. Nonna taught Ava how to properly hold baby birds so she didn't hurt them when it came time each day to weigh them. That night, Nonna knitted a nest out of the softest yarn, and Ava filled it with crumpled tissue. Red especially seemed happiest in the nest, content to snuggle against the already bigger Hazel.

By the third day, Cody MacDonald came calling on her. He stood on the front porch picking at a knot in the wood. "I wanted to tell you I'm off."

"What do you mean, you're off?" Ava said, still in her pajamas. She rubbed her eyes. "I thought you were staying all summer?"

"No, not off, off. We're just off to fish some other lakes. We'll be gone for four days if the weather holds up. Did you know there's all these locks and stuff connecting a million of these lakes? Anyway, I just wanted to tell you."

"Okay," Ava said, unable to help yawning. She leaned her head against the doorframe and closed her eyes. The hot sun felt good on her face.

"Wait," Cody said, stepping back. "Are you sick or something? You don't look so good."

"No, I'm just really tired. Hazel and Red hatched. I'd show you if you had the time."

"You kidding me? I got plenty of time!"

Ava straightened and pulled back her uncombed hair. "I thought you just said you're going on a fishing trip?"

"Yeah, but my dad said we're not leaving for like twenty more minutes."

21

Ava had Cody wash his hands before seeing Hazel and Red. In the corner of the living room, the two birds held their mouths open, their eyes closed, but ready to eat. Cody leaned into the crate, his jaw slack, in awe. "They're just leaving the mouths open all day like that? That looks ridiculous. They must be starving."

"They *always* do that," Ava explained. She reached for Hazel with a soft cloth. "But it's not time to feed them yet. Do you want to help me weigh them?"

"All right," Cody said. Ava wrapped the cloth around Hazel's wings and slowly lifted her out of the crate, just as Nonna had showed her. She carefully placed the three-day-old bird in Cody's hands.

"Don't squeeze," she warned.

"Don't squeeze," Cody repeated. "Got it."

Ava didn't pull her hands away until she could trust that Cody was doing it right. She opened his fingers a little more. "There," she said. "Just keep like that and put Hazel on the scale."

The moment Ava let go, Cody held his breath. "What's wrong?" Ava asked.

"Sorry, I'm a little freaked out that I'm going to hurt it. I don't know if I can do this."

Ava helped Cody place Hazel on the scale. She never imagined he'd be so nervous.

"Fifteen grams?" Cody questioned, reading the scale. "Is that bad?"

"I don't think so. It's more than yesterday. Nonna said they're fine if they keep gaining weight. You can take her off the scale now."

Cody threw up his hands. "You do it. One time was enough for me."

"Okay." Ava couldn't help but smile. Cody wasn't his usual self, acting crazy all the time, telling her what to do. Instead, he sat quietly watching her as she switched out Hazel and put Red carefully on the scale.

"You're much better at that than me," he admitted to her.

"Thanks." Ava wrote down ten grams on the sheet of paper and picked up Red. "Red grew five grams since yesterday. Good job, Red."

Ava placed Red back in the knitted nest Nonna had made. The moment Red settled in, Hazel spread out her wings, draping them around Red, and then Red did the same. It looked as though the two were hugging each other, but Ava wasn't sure if that was true. Either way, Cody and Ava laughed.

"It's pretty cool they have each other like that," Cody said.

"Yeah. I guess it is." They were all quiet for a moment, even the two hungry birds. Ava wasn't sure why, but somehow the silence was slightly embarrassing, and the lamplight felt suddenly warm on her face.

"Don't you have a fishing trip to go to?" Ava said, standing up.

"Yeah, I guess so." Cody sighed. He stumbled to his feet and headed to the door. "My dad keeps saying he's not going to let me take out the Beast if I keep running off without telling him. He's going to have a fit about this."

"Why? Didn't you even tell him you were coming over here?"

"Not *exactly*, but it's not like it's a mystery either," he said. Cody stepped out onto the porch and pointed with both arms at the dock. "He just has to come outside, and he'll see that the Beast is parked right here."

He kicked on his flip-flops and took off down the steps. It was as if being outside had turned Cody back to his old self. "Okay!" he shouted. "See you later, gator. I'll be back next week!"

"Later, gator?" Ava repeated, hearing Cody running along the dock.

"Bye, Mrs. Amato!" she heard him shout.

Nonna walked in to remind Ava it was time to prepare another meal, but Ava had already begun to sterilize the syringes. "I just weighed them," she told Nonna. "Can you check my notebook to see if I'm doing it right?"

"Sure," Nonna said, looking the notebook over. "Was it fun having Cody over?"

"I guess so," Ava said, trying to hold back a smile.

"Good," Nonna said. She kissed Ava on the forehead and handed her back her notebook. "Everything looks perfect."

22

For the rest of the week Ava didn't leave the cabin. She kept beside Hazel and Red and figured out how to use both hands at the same time to feed them so that they didn't peck at each other. She learned to take out the sacs of poop as soon as they appeared and keep clean crumpled tissues inside the nest.

"Wash your hands" was Nonna's advice for everything. Nothing went near the birds that wasn't cleaned first. There was no preparing big batches of food for the countless meals ahead. It had to be made fresh, just as Nonna made fresh pasta for Ava.

Most importantly, ever since the day Hazel and Red were born, her mother's health had improved. There was no more going to the hospital, and her mother told her that she didn't feel as sick in the mornings. The nurses who came to check on her each day had told her that even though the twins inside of her wanted to come out earlier than they should, they were all doing well. Her father used the word *stable* to describe her mother's condition. Stable. That was a word Ava loved. To Ava, stable meant back to normal. It meant back to the way things used to be, as if time were going in reverse.

In a strange way, her mother and she were together again. Both were housebound, so they talked on the phone throughout the day, spending whatever time they could together. Her mother would often say how much older she sounded. However, Ava didn't feel older at all. It was only that she felt the world was making sense again, or as much sense as it had before all the hospital visits and the thought of her mother being in danger was too impossible for her to imagine.

"I just wanted to let you know I'm not mad at you for sending me away," Ava told her mother one night. "I know you just want me to enjoy the summer."

"Well, thank you," her mother answered. "I hope you really are enjoying it."

"I am," Ava said quietly. "But aren't you worried sometimes? You've been in the hospital so much."

"I think it sounds scarier than it is," her mother answered. "It's different when it's happening to you. It's actually quite boring. But it's all worth it. You know, you'll be a big sister soon with two brothers. Two boys. Can you believe it? How do you feel about that?"

"I don't know," Ava answered, feeling awful. "Can we talk about something else?"

"I do talk about them a lot, don't I? Well, what are we going to talk about then? Who's this boy, Cody, you keep mentioning? Let's talk about that. You two seem to be good friends."

"I wouldn't say friends," Ava said, not wanting to discuss him either. "And I don't mention him that much. He's just around, that's all. Well, he's not around right now, actually. Right now, he's on a fishing trip."

"I see."

"Is Dad home?" Ava said, trying to avoid the discussion. "I wanted to say good night to him."

It was late enough in the evening that Ava knew her dad was home. "Tell me everything," he said, answering without even a hello. "What happened today?"

"I don't know," Ava said with a laugh, unsure of where to start. "Well, I learned that the stomach of a bird is five percent of its body weight, and Nonna showed me how to weigh Hazel and Red. Did you know that's the only way to be sure how much to feed them?"

"With how many birds your Nonna took care of over the years, you'd think I'd remember that. But I've forgotten. What else did you do today? Did you get to go out on the canoe?"

"Not today," Ava answered, which only encouraged her dad to go on.

For an hour, he listed everything he could remember, all his favorite coves he'd canoe to when he was her age. He explained which streams led to other lakes and went on about where Ava could still find beaver dams and the quiet places where loons like to nest.

Ava put the phone on the floor while she listened. She was on the verge of sleep when her dad caught her drifting.

"It's late," he said to her. "And I'm talking your ear off. We'll talk more another time."

"No," Ava answered, begging him to continue.

She wanted to talk to him all night, until she had fallen asleep, but Nonna came over to tell her it was time to get off the phone. Ava did as she was told but got upset about it and ended up in tears. Nonna shook her head.

"Ava, it's a party line. Other people might need to use the phone tonight. You should think of that instead of getting mad at me."

The next night, Ava went to bed early, but no matter how hard she tried, she couldn't fall asleep. She was surprised that her mind kept wandering back to Cody MacDonald. She wondered how he was doing on his fishing trip. In their own ways, she reasoned, they were too busy to hang out with each other anymore. She thought about what her mother had said, asking if the two of them were good friends, and Ava still couldn't decide.

In another week, the MacDonalds would pack up and

they'd be gone forever. Ava would leave soon after, she imagined. Nonna still wanted to invite the MacDonalds to dinner before they left. Ava didn't know exactly how to feel about it. Her mind went back and forth in a nervous jumble about having them over.

"It's not a big deal," she said to herself, turning over in her bed. She didn't want to think about Cody MacDonald anymore. Besides, she didn't invite him over. Nonna did. It had nothing to do with her.

23

"You see?" Nonno said to Mr. MacDonald after dinner. They were all still seated around the table when her grandfather showed him a coat hanger that he had bent into a boxlike shape. "Your very own toaster. No need to buy one. You just place it on the burner and a piece of bread goes on top. I made one for Ava too."

"We could have used this when we were camping, that's for sure," Mr. MacDonald said with a laugh.

Ava looked on, slightly embarrassed, but Mr. MacDonald seemed interested. Even the table that they sat around had been carved by her grandfather. This had always struck Ava as somewhat shameful, because perhaps they couldn't afford a nice table from a store.

"Come on," Cody said, elbowing Ava. "Let me see the robins one more time."

"Good idea," Ava said, glad that Cody had asked. Ava and Cody left the table to visit the orange crate that held the two birds. They sat next to each other in the living room. Ava picked up the two birds and held them in her arms.

It had been a week since their hatching. Hazel and Red had most of their feathers and were strong enough to perch upright, though they were clumsy about it. Hazel was more capable and had just started to eat on her own. Red, who had turned out to be a boy, had dark speckled feathers and was growing bigger than Hazel with each day. Still, he preferred to tuck his head under Hazel's wing. Hazel was the first to do everything, being a day older. Wherever Hazel moved, Red followed.

"Look," Cody said. "I told you they'd poop all over you if you hold them. I said it the moment I got here."

"Ugh," Ava moaned. "Can't they stop going to the bathroom for one minute?"

"They're babies," Nonna answered. "All babies do is eat and poop. None of us was any different."

Cody leaned in close to the bird dropping, with more interest than Ava could understand. He started laughing. "It stinks so bad!"

"What did you think it would smell like?" Ava said.

"Wait, let me see that." Nonna came back from the kitchen with a toothpick. She ran the toothpick through the stool and brought it up to her nose. "It shouldn't be so runny. And you're right, Cody, the smell is off."

"See," Cody said, grinning. "I got a good nose for that kind of stuff."

"Congratulations," Ava replied. "You're the king of poop."

"We'll have to take them to the shelter," Nonna continued. "They could be fighting something. Both of them."

"What do you mean?" Ava cradled Hazel and Red close to her.

"We caught it early, so everything should be fine." Nonna went to the kitchen sink and washed her hands. "Sorry. This isn't the most pleasant talk after a meal."

"Not to worry," Mr. MacDonald said, standing up. "That was a wonderful dinner. Thank you. Better than anything I've cooked all summer. Cody, you still okay to drive in the dark alone?"

"You took two boats to come here?" Nonno asked.

"I just got lights put on the Beast!" Cody said, kicking on his shoes. "Tonight's the first night I get to try them out."

"Ava," Nonno said. "Speaking of light, why don't you walk the MacDonalds down to the dock with the flashlight? It's dark going down the steps."

Ava placed Hazel and Red carefully back in their crate. All the while they were reaching out for her, stretching their necks, crying for their mother as any baby would. The two birds looked perfectly fine to her, but suddenly nothing was fine. They were sick and it was her job to care for them, and she hadn't even noticed it. "Did you hear from mom today?" Ava asked her grandmother. "Maybe I should give her a call?"

"You can phone them later if you like," Nonna said. "Now, be careful getting down to the dock."

Ava grabbed one of the many flashlights and showed

the MacDonalds out. She could still hear Hazel and Red calling after her, their voices amplified in the darkness.

Down at the shoreline, the air was cool and damp, and their every step along the dock made a loud splashing sound across the water. "You've got to go first, Dad," Cody said impatiently. "I can't test my lights if you're driving next to me."

"Fair enough," Mr. MacDonald said. "Make sure you put on that life jacket. Good night, Ava."

Cody slipped on his life jacket, damp from the night air, and waited until the bright lights and the grumble of his father's twin engines faded off into the distance. "Okay, here we go," Cody said, climbing into the Beast. He fiddled in the darkness until a little red-and-green light turned on at the front of the bow. "Success!"

He started up his boat but didn't drive away. Instead, he just sat there, staring back at Ava.

"I have to get back," Ava said. "I want to call my mom and make sure everything is okay."

"For sure," Cody answered, still lingering for no reason she could understand. "I hope your mom is okay, really I do."

"Thanks," Ava said, realizing he wasn't just teasing her but meant it sincerely. "Well, I should probably get going."

"I guess so," he said, scratching his arm. Ava couldn't figure out what had gotten into him. A bat flew right by them just then, skimming the water for bugs, and for some reason neither one of them said a word about it.

Instead, the little green-and-red light just kept bobbing up and down, casting up at their faces as they looked at each other. Being with Cody felt different to Ava at night than it did in the day. Perhaps, she wondered, that's why he was looking at her so strangely. She thought that maybe he'd felt that too.

Finally, Cody just pulled away from the dock without a word. When he was out past where Ava could see him, she heard him stop the engine.

"Well, you already know it's my last week here, and then we're packing up and going home and that's that, and, you know, I just wanted to tell you I'm going to miss hanging out with you, Ava Amato!"

Ava went completely still. Cody had blurted out these words all at once as if he were trying to win a contest to see who could say the most words in the shortest amount of time.

He started up his boat again and drove off without saying another word. It was a relief to Ava that he left right then. She didn't know what to make of what he had said, or what she would have said back to him if he had stuck around.

She waited under the flood of stars while Cody MacDonald's green-and-red light slowly made its way across the bay. When he was safely docked, the lake was quiet. In the dim yellow porch light, Ava caught one more glimpse of him, making his way up the dock.

24

Ava rubbed her eyes. The morning was bright, and her room felt extra stuffy and warm. But she had slept so deeply that she felt weak. It reminded her of the time when she had had the flu and slept for the whole day, her strength returning only after she had gotten up from her bed.

The living room was quiet, and the windows and curtains were open. Outside, the lake was as smooth as glass. The clock radio read 11:16, and there was a note waiting for her on the kitchen table.

We didn't want to wake you. At the shelter. Make yourself some breakfast. We'll be home before lunch.

Love, Nonna and Nonno

Ava tried not to worry as she cut a thick, jagged piece of bread and placed it on the coat-hanger toaster that her grandfather had made for her. She lit the burner until the flame fluttered upward in a blue ring, and, once the bread was toasted, Ava spread on rhubarb jam and ate the whole piece standing by the stove. She was suddenly starving. She cut a second, thicker slice and took it to the dock. Between bites, she used the binoculars to look straight across the bay, her eyes fixed on the marina parking lot, waiting for her grandparents' car to appear.

By the time Ava finished her second piece of toast, her body brimmed with energy. She wanted to do something, anything to pass the time until Hazel and Red returned. She brushed her crumbs into the lake and watched the tiny silver fish appear from under the dock to nibble them.

She took the broom from under the stairwell and swept, starting on the top deck, working her way down, clearing out the old cobwebs from the cracks between logs. Still there was no sign of her grandparents, and so she canoed to the small dock and pulled the tomatoes into the sun. She went inside to call her parents, but they didn't answer, so she watered the garden, taking special care of the sweet potatoes, weeding out all the clovers from the sandy soil, surprised by how much the leaves had already grown.

It was around lunchtime when Cody appeared.

"Hey, who are you spying on?" he said, pulling up to the dock.

"I'm waiting for Hazel and Red," she said, not looking away from the binoculars.

"That's so boring! It's my last week here, remember? You have to go fishing with me at least once."

Cody waved two fishing rods at Ava, but Ava wasn't listening. A boat was approaching in the distance. Ava refocused the binoculars, finding it easier to close one eye and look through the binoculars like a telescope. It was her grandparents' boat.

"They're back!" Ava shrieked. "Hazel! Red! I'm coming!" She tossed Cody the binoculars and dove from the dock, swimming toward them as hard as she would in any swim meet.

"Wait!" Cody cried. "It'll be faster if you take the

Beast!" But Ava had already left Cody behind, coming out from the water in a butterfly stroke. "Geez, you swim fast!" he called. By the time Cody had turned the boat and caught up, Ava had already grabbed hold of the side rail of her grandparents' boat.

"Where's Hazel and Red?" she said, out of breath. "How are they? What happened?"

"They're keeping them for a few days for observation," Nonna answered. "They needed some antibiotics. Nothing more. My goodness, you're swimming in your pajamas!"

"When can I go and see them?"

"Unfortunately, no one can. But they should be fine."

"*Should* be?" Ava repeated, letting go of the boat and kicking backward.

"Yes. Should be. Oh, and look what came in the mail."

Nonna pulled a letter from her purse. The letter was addressed to Ava in her mother's cursive. "I'll leave it on the dock. When you're done reading it, you can help Nonno convert the screen porch into an aviary. Those two birds will have to live out there from now on. We can't have fledglings flying loose all around the house.

They'll get hurt. Cody, are you staying for lunch?"

"Yes, please!" he cried.

"Okay. We'll see you two at home."

Their boat puttered away.

"But isn't it bad luck to have a bird flying around the house?" Ava called out after them.

Nonna looked back at her. "Ava, they've been in the house with us all this time. For the millionth time, nothing bad is going to happen. Now enjoy your swim. Lunch will be on the picnic table in ten minutes!"

25

Under the dappled light of the sugar maples, Nonno, Cody, and Ava emptied the screen porch of furniture. Nonno showed them how to build a perch out of birchwood and cover one side of the porch with maple branches so that the broad leaves were a nice shade from the afternoon sun.

"Good," Nonno said, handing Ava the last nail. "One more and this perch will be nice and steady."

Ava hammered the nail until it disappeared into the wood.

"Bravo. Now feel around and make sure nothing

sticks out. There can't be anything for those two young birds to cut themselves on."

"Feels good to me," Ava replied. Touching the soft peeling branches of the gray birch felt like running her hands through the pages of a book.

"Are you sure it's safe for them in here?" Ava asked. "Couldn't a bear come through the screen and eat them?"

"A bear could come through the front door if it wanted and eat us," Nonno said. "But no, not likely if we keep their food sealed and the place clean. If anything, we have to watch out for raccoons."

"Bears and raccoons?" Cody said, looking around the trees. "On an island? No way."

"Anything that wants to make its way onto this island can if it likes." Nonno took the hammer from Ava's hands. "Did you like your mother's letter?"

"Yes. Dad says he's proud of me for raising Hazel and Red. And Mom says she misses me. She says she has no one to eat nurungji with her. Stuff like that."

"Do you want to make something for your brothers

123

too? I have plenty of old wood in the shed. We could make a playpen or a pair of rocking horses. Anything you think they'd like."

"Brothers?" Cody said. "I know exactly what they'd want! We should make them a bow and arrow or a rocket launcher! Something like that!"

The smile left Ava's face. "No, I don't think so," she said quietly. She didn't want to talk about bows and arrows or rocket launchers. She wanted to change the subject. "Nonno, when do you think Hazel and Red will be home?"

"It's like the twins. They'll be coming any day now. If we can count on anything, we can count on that." Nonno picked up the scraps of wood and turned to go. "If you change your mind about making your brothers something, call me."

Just then the phone rang.

"Ava!" Nonna called from inside. "It's your mother."

"Hold on a sec," Ava said to Cody. Ava returned to the porch with the cordless phone.

"Hi, Mrs. Amato!" Cody yelled into the receiver.

Ava pushed Cody away. "Mom," she said, turning her back to him. "How are you? I tried to call but no one answered . . . Who?" Ava looked Cody up and down. "No, that's nobody."

Cody made a face, but Ava ignored him. She was too busy listening to her mother explain how she was back in the hospital, but she assured Ava that everything was okay. Her mother only wanted to talk to Ava about her brothers. How one of her brothers didn't move all that much, but the one on top, who was smaller, kicked so constantly that her mother was sure he wanted out. The doctor said it would be better if they came out a little later, as they were still small, though her mother laughed and told Ava they certainly didn't feel small.

"Are you doing anything fun today?" her mother asked. "Any day now you'll have two little brothers. I was wondering what you think their names should be. Do you want to help me choose their names?"

"No, thanks, but I'm fine if you're fine," Ava answered.

"But are you sure you're fine? You're back in the hospital again. It must be serious."

"Ava, I'm fine," her mother said in a tired voice. "I didn't call to worry you. I just thought you might want to help me pick names for the boys."

Cody kept trying to lean toward the phone and listen, and each time Ava pushed him away. She wasn't in the mood for any of his jokes.

"Sorry, Ava, I'd better go. The nurse is here to run more tests. I love you."

"Okay. I love you too. Call me tonight so I know you're okay." Ava hung up the phone and lay down on the floor. She stared out onto the lake. "I knew it. As soon as Hazel and Red get sick, my mom ends up back in the hospital."

"What does that have to do with anything?"

"How many times do I have to tell you? I'm *cursed*."

"Okay," Cody groaned. "You're cursed. Sorry, I forgot. Now can we just go and do something? You can come up to the lake anytime you like, but it's my last week here, remember?"

Ava rolled onto her back and closed her eyes. "I don't feel like doing anything today. And stop reminding me that you're leaving all the time. I know it's your last week. I remembered the first hundred times you told me."

"Well, you don't act like you remember," Cody answered.

Ava stared at the water.

"Why don't you just tell me about the curse? I don't ever know what you're talking about."

Ava looked up at Cody. It wasn't like she felt good about hiding the curse from him. A part of her really did want to tell him, if only for him to know the seriousness of the situation. The more Ava thought about it, the more she was sure that if she explained the curse to Cody he'd understand. It felt strange to think it, but she trusted to tell him about the curse more than anyone else.

"Hello, Earth to Ava. Earth to Ava," Cody said with a laugh. "Really, why are you staring at me like that? You're acting so weird."

"I am not," Ava said. "I was just thinking about something, okay?"

"So we're *not* doing anything today."

Ava was too annoyed with him now to answer.

"Fine." Cody peered out the screen porch. "I guess I can forget about hanging out with you. Where's your grandfather? Maybe he can show me how to make that rocket launcher."

"Great idea," Ava mumbled.

Ava lay there listening as the screen door slammed shut. She heard Cody wandering the garden below until eventually he gave up on finding her grandfather and got in his boat and drove away. She wondered if Cody would forget her when he went back to school. She wasn't even sure she'd tell her friend Ruby about him. If she did, how would she begin to describe him? Every time Ava imagined telling Ruby, it came out a different way. Nothing felt right to her, and the more Ava tried to think of how to explain it, the sillier she felt about the whole thing.

The wake from Cody's boat reached the shoreline and splashed along the rocks. Ava held still, listening until the waves calmed and the only noise beyond the swaying trees was Nonna doing something in the kitchen.

How could she begin to explain to anyone how much she needed her mother? She needed her more than she needed twin brothers or rocking chairs or spending the last days of Cody MacDonald's vacation fishing. Ava felt terrible for thinking such things, but deep down it was the truth. And her mother had been doing fine right up to the moment Hazel and Red got sick. Now there was nothing Ava could do but wait.

"Do you want to help me choose their names?" Ava repeated her mother's words in her mind until a sense of nausea came over her.

When Ava imagined her mother calling her from that hospital bed, she always saw her in a plain cotton gown with colored wires connected everywhere and all sorts of awful beeping and the team of doctors around her. Maybe that's not how it actually was, Ava thought, but she was old enough to know that when you're sent to the hospital, it's for a reason.

She swore to herself that the next time she hung out with Cody MacDonald, she'd take him to the island and tell him about the curse. What other choice did she

have? She was running out of time. *And who knows?* Ava thought. *Cody might even know a way out of all this.*

Ava draped her arm over her head and blocked the sun from her eyes. "Any day now," she moaned. That was all everyone kept saying to her. "Any day now" whatever was about to happen would happen. No matter if the outcome was good or bad, all Ava knew for sure was her life would never be the same.

26

Ava spent the next morning glued to Nonna's side, waiting for news from the shelter and for her mother to return her call. Nonna kept busy at the picnic table, snapping open the fava shells and tossing the flat beans she found inside into a pot. That morning, she had taught Ava how to string hot peppers with a needle and thread and how to braid the stems of onions together. They lay in great bundles across the picnic table.

"You'll have to take the ones you made home," Nonna said. "The peppers from those seeds we got from your mother."

Everyone in their own way was preparing for the babies to be born. Ava tried not to think about it and laid her head on the table. Her skin felt sticky in the heat.

"That's enough for one morning," Nonna said, slowly straightening. It was the first time Ava had ever seen Nonna look tired.

"I'll finish it," Ava said, prying open the last few fuzzy shells to collect the beans inside. Nonno nodded and Ava could tell Nonna's mind was somewhere else. The closer it came to the birth, the quieter her grandparents became, silently going about whatever work needed to be done.

The familiar boom from the building of the new road echoed across the lake, though it was less frequent and came from farther away. Still, Ava had not completely gotten used to it. She picked up the binoculars and climbed the stairs. A half dozen deer were swimming across the bay, making their way from the mainland to Deer Island.

"That construction is scaring those poor deer," Ava complained. "I wish it would stop."

"I like it about as much as they do," Nonna answered, getting up. "Why don't you call Cody? You won't have time when Hazel and Red return. Maybe take a boat ride to the island or something."

"The island?" Ava hesitated. "I think I should wait here. What if the shelter calls?"

"I'll phone them at the end of the day and find out. Look, I can see the MacDonalds' boat from here. They're home."

Ava focused the binoculars. Cody was on the dock, polishing the side of the Beast with a thick blue rag. He was dancing to a portable radio that Ava could faintly hear.

"I don't know," Ava said, the binoculars growing heavy. "He looks busy to me."

Cody stood up and threw the rag over his shoulder, admiring his work, and then, without any warning, leaned down and kissed his boat.

"Augh." Ava cringed. "What's wrong with him?"

"Wrong with who?" Nonna said, taking up the pot of beans.

Cody MacDonald must have had a sense that he was being watched. He looked up from his boat and stared directly back at Ava. He didn't seem to mind at all that Ava was spying on him. Instead, he hopped to his feet and waved his arms wildly in the air.

"Him," Ava answered, putting the binoculars to her side. "What's wrong with *him?*"

27

"This is all you wanted to show me?" Cody groaned, standing over the feather that marked the woodpecker's grave. "What's dangerous about that?"

"What's dangerous is this is why I'm cursed," Ava said, annoyed. "You asked, and I'm finally showing you."

Cody picked up the feather. "Well, can we at least dig up the bones and see it?"

"No," Ava said, carefully placing the feather back. "That's disgusting. Besides, I think this whole place might be cursed."

"No way. I've been here a thousand times. This island is too boring to be cursed." Cody looked around, disappointed.

"And this whole time, I was thinking you had a real curse."

"My mother is back in the hospital. That's real enough for me."

"Okay, okay. You told me about the bird dying and curse thing. So what are you going to do now?"

"There's nothing to do. I told you, we made a deal."

"You made a deal with a dead bird?"

"Yes, but I can't tell you about that part. It's really an awful thing to say."

Cody smiled, as though what Ava had said was the most exciting thing that had happened to him all day. "Now we're talking! Just tell me. Please tell me!"

Ava looked back at him reluctantly. "It's too bad. I can't say it out loud. You have to come closer."

Cody leaned in closer, grinning.

"All I said was . . . you can take them, but you just can't take her."

"That's not so bad . . . Who's them?"

Ava cupped her hands against his ear and explained in a whisper the awful promise she had made. The smile left

Cody's face and his skin went a chalky white.

"What! Are you kidding me? That *is* bad. You know you can't say stuff like that, don't you?"

"I know, but you don't understand."

"I'd never promise that. Not even to a dumb old dead bird! You gotta take it back!"

Ava's face hardened. *What does he know about it?* she thought. "I won't take it back. And besides, that's not how curses work. And you're acting like I had another choice. Like I'm just being mean for no reason!"

"You always have a choice!"

"That's easy for you to say!" Ava said, her fists trembling. "You came up her for a stupid fishing trip. Your mother is fine."

"That doesn't matter, Ava. I'm serious. You have to take it back. Like, right now."

"It *does* matter," Ava said. She took a deep breath, not wanting to cry in front of Cody MacDonald, not wanting to admit how scared she was about everything. "That's all that matters. Don't you see?"

She expected Cody to argue with her, but instead he

was quiet, blinking hard as he stared at her. Ava realized then she should never have brought him to the cove and shared what she had done. It was her fault for telling him, she said to herself, for trusting him like a real friend and admitting to him things she'd never told anyone in the entire world.

"Fine," Ava lied to him. "I'll take it back." Cody looked instantly relieved. Ava couldn't understand how he'd believe her so suddenly. She felt she had no choice but to keep on pretending, leading him along. "Okay. I just took back everything, just like you said. Can we go now?"

His whole face brightened. Whatever burden he once felt seemed to have completely lifted.

"Come on," he said, running to his boat. "Let's forget about this place and do something that's actually fun."

They pushed the boat free from the reeds and dropped the engine, but the happier Cody seemed to be, the worse Ava felt. The only reason she had taken him there was because she thought it would help to tell someone about the curse. She knew Nonna was certainly done talking about it with her. She thought by telling Cody he'd understand and take her side, but he didn't take her side at all. Instead, he made her feel sick about the whole thing.

"Hey, check this out!" he said, laughing. The boat drifted as Cody shoved his arm in front of Ava. A mosquito had landed on his forearm. "Here, I'll show you what an actual curse looks like. This mosquito is about to be cursed, by me!"

He pinched the skin around the mosquito, giggling like a crazy person. "Gotcha! The drink-till-you-explode curse has been cast. Now what will you do? You'll just have to keep drinking and drinking and drinking until you explode."

"That mosquito's biting you," she mumbled, half interested.

"Yes, but don't you see? If you pinch your skin hard enough, it can't let go. I'm holding its stinger in place. It's stuck."

Ava watched the mosquito, wondering if it was in as much trouble as Cody said it was in. In the end, the mosquito didn't explode. Instead, it got big and round until it opened its wings and flew lazily away.

"Oh, man!" he said, rubbing his arm. "I guess I wasn't holding on to it tight enough."

"Aren't you going to have a huge bite now?"

Cody looked down at the bite. It had already swollen up to the size of a quarter. "I don't think so."

"Why did you do that?" Ava said, still mad at him. "I don't understand you sometimes."

Cody kept on rubbing his bite. "I don't know. I guess I was just trying to cheer you up."

Ava put on her life jacket and slumped down at the front of the boat. "I should head back. I want to be there when the shelter or my mom calls."

"What? At least give me a turn to do something fun after you dragged me to this rock pile! Besides, who knows when they'll call?" Cody turned the throttle all the way, kicking the Beast into a steady crawl.

"Wait, where are we going?" Ava protested. "My grandparents' place is that way."

"I don't know where I'm going! That's my point! Look!" Cody shut off the motor and put his hands behind his head. "Let's just drift. We'll just see where the water takes us. It could be fun! What's the worst that can happen?"

Ava pointed toward the shore. "We'll end up over there. Smashed up against those rocks. Is that what you want?"

Cody looked to where Ava was pointing and sighed. "Fine. I got another idea," he said, starting back up the engine. "You out of all people will love it. It's always sunny and comes with a diving board."

"A diving board?" Ava said, unable to help being a little curious.

Cody directed the Beast headlong into the wind. On the open lake, the Beast was slower than any other boat Ava could imagine, but Cody just smiled at Ava and rubbed his hand over the engine. It was the happiest Ava had ever seen him.

"Go! Beast! Go!" he kept chanting, chasing after the small patch of sun.

28

"Are you jumping in or what?" Cody sang out. "The sun's going to disappear any second, and we'll have to drive to another spot." Ava was standing at the bow of Cody's boat in the middle of the lake, looking down at the dark water.

"I'm going to, but this isn't much of a diving board." Ava lifted her arms and bent her knees, and the boat rocked up and down. The moment Ava jumped into the air she knew that it wasn't her greatest dive. She entered the water at too shallow an angle.

"See," Cody said, kicking up his feet onto the side of his boat and placing his hands behind his head. "Don't tell me this doesn't beat swimming off the dock. Out here we can go anywhere we like."

"I guess," Ava called from the water. "Aren't you going to swim?"

Cody shook his head proudly. "Water safety. That's the number one rule of having a boat. A captain always stays with his ship."

"That's a dumb rule. And don't you have to have an actual ship to be called a captain?"

"I don't think so. Hey, are you going to come back here next summer? I really think I can convince my dad. I could work a summer job at the marina, fixing boats."

"What do you know about repairing boats?" Ava said, swimming closer.

"Nothing, but I can park boats or pump gas while they teach me."

"We're eleven. I don't think we're allowed to work."

"And next year I'll be twelve, so I'm sure they'd let it slide. Can't you be a lifeguard? With all this water, that's got to be a job."

"You have to be way older than twelve to be a lifeguard,"

Ava explained. "There's a bunch of tests. And you have to know CPR and stuff like that."

"I'd rather work at the marina. Kissing old people all day sounds for sure like the worst job ever."

"CPR isn't kissing anyone," Ava said, floating on her back. "You're breathing into their lungs."

"Whatever. Your lips are touching. That's kissing."

The sliver of sun disappeared behind the clouds and Ava was instantly cold. "I think I'm done," she said, climbing back into the boat. The late afternoon air left goosebumps on her skin.

"One more dive? We can head to another sun spot if you like?"

"Maybe another time." Ava shivered, grabbing a towel from under the seat. "It's getting close to dinner."

"But I still have a full tank of gas."

"Maybe tomorrow," Ava said, knowing Cody was disappointed.

They drove back toward their bay, not saying a word to each other. Ava sat at the bow so the hull didn't get knocked around so much in the waves. The wind died the moment they were back in the protected bay, and Cody's boat picked up speed. The water was so smooth that Ava could see the reflection of cottages and trees just as clearly as if she were looking directly at them. "Deer like to swim to that island," Ava said, wanting to break the silence between them.

"I've seen those deer plenty of times," Cody grumbled, refusing to look at her. Ava gave up. There was no helping the fact that he was mad at her. All Cody MacDonald ever wanted to do was spend the day on his boat, she thought to herself, and she was tired of it.

As they rounded the island, they saw Nonno on the dock, reading. Cody cut the engine well before they reached the place. Ava knew he was showing off in front of her grandfather, letting the boat coast the rest of the way so that it glided in, parking just perfectly against the dock. It was clear to Ava that he had been practicing, but she wasn't in the mood to compliment him on it.

"Nice driving," Nonno said, putting down his book.

"Did anyone call?" Ava interrupted, but Nonno didn't have to answer. Ava looked up to see the two robins flying around the screen porch, singing.

Ava leapt from the boat. "Hazel! Red! They're home!" She took off up the dock.

"Go on with her if you like," Nonno told Cody. "I'll tie down the boat for you. That's your aviary too. You helped build it."

Cody smiled wide and nodded. "Thanks. Hey, Ava! Wait up!" But Ava wasn't listening.

"They're home!" she cried, racing into the screen porch. "I can't believe they're home!"

29

The weekend had arrived, as hot and humid as ever. Ava had spent the last two days lying inside the makeshift aviary, staring up at Hazel and Red as they moved from perch to perch and foraged in the leaves where Ava had hid thimbleberries or dug for earthworms in the shallow bowls left on the floor.

"They can fly around perfectly now," Ava said. "They're really getting the hang of it."

"I know," Cody said with a sigh. "We've been watching them fly around for like forever." He pressed his nose against the screen door. "You said we were going fishing, remember?"

"Look! Red found it!" Ava had hung a piece of broccoli from a stick that Red especially liked to nibble on.

"It's my last weekend, and you know it. Yesterday you said I could pick, and I picked fishing right behind your place. We can even walk there."

"Well, I take it back, okay? I have to take care of Hazel and Red. You know that."

"What's to take care of? Look how big they are now. They probably hate being trapped in this porch. Why don't you just let them go?"

"Let them go?" The thought had never crossed her mind. "If I let them out, they may never come back."

Ava pushed past Cody and called for her grandmother. "Nonna! If we let Hazel and Red outside, won't they fly away?"

Nonna squinted up from the garden. "Letting them fly away wouldn't be such a bad thing, would it? They're growing up."

"But I don't want them to go. I love them."

Nonna picked the last of the zucchini flowers and came up the stairs. "Ava, just because you love them doesn't mean they'll stay with us forever. They can hunt for food by themselves now. Soon they'll want to leave."

"You're right, Mrs. Amato," Cody said. "I did a project on robins once. A robin never returns to its nest."

Cody was being so unhelpful that Ava wondered if he was doing it on purpose, just to hurt her. "That's not the same thing," she argued. "I'm their mother. They're *my* birds."

"Ava," Nonna said. "They're not yours. Nothing in nature is ours to keep."

"But I have to keep them. At least until . . . Can't they stay with you? I can see them whenever I come to visit."

"Really, bella, they belong outside. If you love them as much as you say you do, you know the right thing to do eventually is to let them go free."

Ava kept silent as Nonna went inside. She knew not to say anything about the curse to anyone ever again.

"So are we going fishing or what?" Cody MacDonald asked.

"You could have been more helpful, you know. Why did you have to go saying all that?"

"What did I do?"

"So what if I wanted to keep them? What's the big

deal? Lots of people keep birds. I don't say anything when all you talk about is your stupid boat."

"The Beast isn't stupid. And don't be mad at me. Those birds don't want to live in that jail, and you know it."

"Like I'm going to take advice from someone who makes out with their boat."

To Ava's surprise, Cody didn't say anything at all. He grabbed his fishing rod and walked away. It wasn't until he got down to the dock that he looked back at her.

"You know why you think you're cursed? Because you think everything's about you, that's why. You're selfish! Nothing's going to happen to your mother or you or your brothers. The only problem you have is you're too busy worrying about yourself."

Ava flung open the screen porch door, wanting to make sure he could hear her every word. "Oh yeah?" she shouted back. "Well, we're no longer friends! We were never real friends."

"Big deal!" he said, untying his boat. "I'm leaving in like two days, so what does it matter? We're never going to see each other again!" He got into his boat and lowered his engine.

Ava waited for him to leave, but Cody just kept messing around with his boat. He pulled at all the knobs around the engine and pumped the gas line from his tank, acting to Ava like he had all the time in the world.

"Well, just go already!" Ava demanded.

Cody threw up his arms, looking at her as if she was the dumbest person in the world. *"I am.* But first I got to prime the engine. I'm not going to ruin the Beast because of you!"

Ava's insides were trembling. She couldn't stand to talk to Cody MacDonald a second longer. She rushed back inside and thought to slam the screen porch door behind her so he'd know exactly how mad she was at him, but the porch door caught on the floorboards. Ava tried a second time, and the old door squeaked to a halt.

"Ha!" he laughed, starting his engine. "You can't even slam a door without someone's help!"

"It's not my fault the door sticks!"

"That's right, I forgot! Nothing's your fault. You're just cursed!"

Ava looked down at Cody MacDonald then and in her mind vowed to never speak to him again as long as she lived. She wanted to run to her room but couldn't bear to give him the satisfaction. Instead, she stood in the screen porch with her fist clenched. In another day or two he would be out of her life forever, she told herself. Still, she had to stand there, putting up with Cody MacDonald's boat buzzing along the lake, like an insect flying around her, refusing to go away.

"You're the one who's selfish!" Ava shouted. She waited to see if Cody would dare look back at her. But Cody never looked back, and all Ava could think about is how she was always taking care of Hazel and Red while all Cody was doing was riding around in his boat. She turned to her birds. "Who gets a boat just because their parents are divorced anyway?" she muttered to them. "He's so spoiled!"

While Cody slowly made his way across the bay, the fight between them replayed over and over in Ava's mind. The more Ava thought about it, the more she believed they were never friends in the first place. It left her feeling helpless and, after a while, angry. Angry at everything bad that had happened to her, from her mother being in the hospital to allowing herself to get to know someone as annoying as Cody MacDonald in the first place.

30

Dawn began with a clap of thunder and heavy wind knocking the trees. Ava's room was dark. She could hear the rain beating on the roof above her. She jumped out of bed and went to the screen porch to check on Hazel and Red.

Ava didn't know why, but she stopped before she got to the doorway, sensing small differences before she even understood what it was that had happened. She walked slowly, noticing a small tear in the screen and the smudge of dirt on the floorboards and the puddle of rain around the threshold of the door.

"Hazel?" she whispered. "Red?" She leaned into the

doorway and found the porch room destroyed. The perches and food bins were knocked over. The containers of worms and the sealed bowl of fruit were emptied, and dirt was dumped all over the floor. There was no sign of Hazel and Red. Ava ran back inside.

"Nonna!" Ava said, shaking her grandmother awake. "They're gone! Hazel and Red are gone!"

"Who's gone?" Nonna mumbled, reaching for her glasses.

"Something got into the screen porch!"

Ava led Nonna by the hand.

"Raccoons," Nonna said, pointing to the oily paw prints everywhere. "Look. Around the door."

"They ate them, and it's all my fault! I must have left the screen door open."

Nonna hugged her granddaughter. "It's nobody's fault. Look. No flight feathers anywhere. I'm sure those raccoons were probably too full to bother chasing around a couple birds."

Ava looked up at her grandmother and ran out of the screen porch and into the rain. She stood there in her pajamas, hoping to find Hazel and Red in the trees. "But they wouldn't be safe out there alone," she said, her pajamas getting soaked. "Something is going to eat them. I have to find them."

"Ava, come in out of the rain. For Pete's sake, you're not going to find them in this storm."

Ava squatted down, peering desperately into the nearby brush.

"Ava, listen to me," Nonna said in a gentler voice. "There's not a soul on this earth that doesn't know to take cover in a storm, and that includes those two birds. There's no use in looking for them now. They won't come out."

Ava looked steadily into her grandmother's eyes, eyes that never lied or hid anything from her in her life. Ava's wet pajamas stuck to her skin. "But can't I just look for a little bit?"

"When the rain lets up, we'll go out looking for them. I promise. In the meantime, you can eat some breakfast first and search for them all you like through the window."

Ava's eyes narrowed, studying the dark clouds above. "But when will it stop?"

"I don't know, but it will." Her grandmother stepped out of the porch and into the rain. She took Ava's hand. "Don't worry, a storm can't last forever," she said, leading Ava back inside. "Now let's get you changed, and I'll make you some hot chocolate."

31

Back inside, Ava was pulling on a sweatshirt when Nonno rushed by outside the window wearing a yellow raincoat. "Where's Nonno going?" Ava called, forgetting all about getting changed.

"I'm sure he's going down to the dock to put away whatever needs putting away." Nonna dialed the phone and switched it to speaker.

"Weather conditions at eight a.m.," said the polite voice. "Extreme storm warning in effect for the following regions: Lindsay, Peterborough, Lakefield, Haliburton, Kawartha Lakes. Temperature twenty-nine. Precipitation ninety percent. Winds thirty-two kilometers an hour, gusting up to one hundred kilometers an hour. Barometric pressure one hundred kilopascals. This has been Environment Canada."

"But they didn't say when the storm would be over," Ava complained.

"Ava, please get properly changed," Nonna said, hanging up the phone, but there was no force to her voice. Instead, they both just stood there watching the storm move across the lake. The rain was coming down so hard that the water overflowed the eaves like a curtain.

Ava grabbed the binoculars. Boats from everywhere were speeding into the marina with their covers on and their windshield wipers racing. Cottagers were on their docks, trying to flip over their canoes and chasing anything that needed tying down. Thanks to the wind, flowerpots and deck chairs were flying into the water. Ava spotted a single neon-blue water ski floating in the middle of the bay.

Everyone seemed to have something that belonged to them in that lake, but Ava couldn't find what belonged to her. She searched the tops of the trees, but Hazel and Red weren't there. She spotted Cody MacDonald's dock and dropped the binoculars.

"Nonna! The boats are gone at Cody's place. They're gone!"

"Maybe they've already headed home for the summer," Nonna answered. "Weren't they leaving this weekend?"

"They're leaving tomorrow," Ava explained. "Their car is still in their driveway."

A large tree branch came down onto the roof and shook the cabin. Ava ran for the front door. "I'm going to help Nonno!"

"Good idea," Nonna said, walking to the door. "But you two have to be quick about it."

Ava took off down the steps. Two of the yellow folding chairs slid along the dock, about to blow into the water. "I'll get them!" she shouted to her grandfather over the wind.

"Don't worry about those!" Nonno called back. "They'll sink right where they are. We just don't want to lose the dock." The storm was blowing so heavily across the water that one side of the main dock had come loose and the wind had sent it sideways.

"We have to tie it down," Nonno shouted. Ava grabbed hold of the thick rope attached to the dock and pulled while her grandfather gathered the slack and tied the other end of the rope tightly around a tree.

"Good. That'll hold," he shouted, then waved for her to come along with him. They climbed down the rocks along the shoreline, and Nonno dragged in the small dock of tomato plants right up onto the rocks, driving it under the leaning cedars. The pots were already shattered, and the tomato plants were snapped at their stalks, dragging along in the lake.

Ava looked through the trees, past the white-capped waves, out at the MacDonalds' place. "Cody's boat is gone!"

Nonno blinked against the hard rain. "It probably broke away from the dock. We'll help them look for it after the storm. Here, take these." Nonno handed Ava two canoe paddles. "Come on. Let's get inside."

Ava did all she could to keep the paddles from flying

out of her hands. Water rushed down the steps and carved deep grooves into the earth. It poured from the portico like a waterfall. Ava had never seen anything like it. She paused before going through the falling water. She didn't know why, but it felt to her that if she walked through that water, she'd have no chance of finding Hazel or Red or Cody MacDonald or seeing her mother again. She didn't belong inside. She needed to be out there, looking for them.

"Ava, come on inside!" Nonno called. Her grand-father was looking back at her, and Ava could see that he didn't know what to say or do. But he put his arm around her shoulders and guided her up the front steps. "It's going to be fine," he said. When Ava walked under the roof and felt the water coming down upon them, she started to cry.

"Nonno." Her voice was too weak for him to hear her. She wanted to tell him that even though she and Cody MacDonald weren't friends anymore, she knew he would never have let his boat float off onto the lake. *Not in a million, gazillion years,* she thought. Even if the storm stopped right then, no way would they find Cody

MacDonald at his place. If the Beast was missing, Ava knew, then so was Cody MacDonald.

Ava wanted to tell her grandfather all this, but the words were caught up in her throat. Caught up in that storm. Hazel, Red, and Cody MacDonald were all out there. Ava just knew it.

32

Nonna met them at the door with towels.

"We should call the MacDonalds," Nonno said, shutting the door to keep the storm from coming in behind him. "They'll want to know their boats are missing."

"Good idea," Nonna answered. "Ava, you get changed first and then give Cody a call."

Ava ran to her room, her wet pajamas dripping along the floorboards. She was grabbing a dry set of clothes when, through her bedroom window, she saw a glimpse of Cody rushing up the path to their front door.

"Cody!" Ava yelled, throwing open the window and

leaning out in the heavy rain. "Are you crazy coming over here in this storm?"

Mr. MacDonald turned at the foot of the steps and looked up at Ava in surprise. His red checkered jacket was soaked and slumping off his shoulders, and there was a frightened look in his eyes, like the eyes of a child. Somehow, even with his big, thick walrus mustache, Ava thought it was Cody coming up those steps. Ava had never noticed the resemblance before.

"Have you seen him?" Mr. MacDonald asked, his voice shaking. "Cody, I mean. I thought he might be here?"

Ava didn't know how to answer. She shook her head.

"I see." Mr. MacDonald coughed, rubbing his throat. The rain fell heavier then, as though not from the clouds but from every direction; it came crashing through the air, stinging her cheeks, and leaving pockmarks in the dirt. "I thought for sure he'd come by. His rod was gone, and last night all he could talk about was getting in one more day of fishing. He was gone before I woke up. I shouldn't have let him go alone."

Ava wanted to run inside and get her grandparents but didn't want to leave Mr. MacDonald. She didn't know what to do, so she said the only place she imagined Cody might be. "I think he probably went out digging for worms first. He's got a special place."

Mr. MacDonald wiped his brow, and his voice broke before Ava could understand him. "I know the place . . . I'm sure you're right. Thank you, Ava." He started to turn toward the path that led down to the dock. "I better get going. I'll ring your grandparents when I've found him."

Even after Mr. MacDonald had gone off down to his boat, Ava waited at the window in the rain, thinking about where Cody MacDonald really could be. The rain poured along the windowsill and onto the floorboards until it had puddled at her feet.

She hoped Cody was getting worms just like she said. She closed her eyes, believing if she could see him there clearly in her mind, then maybe what she said was true, and he was hiding out under the thick pines from the storm. Ava was looking up into the swaying trees for any sign of Hazel or Red when the phone rang.

She heard Nonna answer.

Hello? Is that you, Arlo?

Ava rushed to the bedroom phone and brought it to her ear.

Yes, we're all right so far . . . We might lose power. How are things at the hospital? . . . Surgery? . . . Say that again, Arlo. The reception isn't great.

She tried to focus on what her father was saying, but his voice had turned staticky and the line kept crackling.

Don't worry, Mom. The boys . . . fine. Everyone will be . . . The doctors are just . . . and concerned—

Ava tried hard to piece together his words. Words that traveled through a thin phone line, trying to make their way to her through the storm. Words that were being battered by the wind and sank underwater until finally they had reached their tiny island where all that rock seemed to smash what remained into little fragments. Splintered words like *emergency* and *waiting for a second surgeon* were all that made their way through the phone line for Ava to somehow piece together.

Arlo, I missed that. When's surgery? What did the doctors say? The room was spinning, and Ava could no longer understand. Her father's voice was muffled and dim.

Can you still hear me, Arlo?

The cordless fell from Ava's hands. It hit the floor and the batteries scattered under the bed.

Arlo?

The power in the cabin went out and Ava's room went dark.

"Ava?" Nonna called from behind the door. "I need to talk to you." Nonna knocked but didn't wait to enter. She found Ava's room empty and the phone broken on the floor. The bedroom curtains blew back in the wind. The storm rushed in through the open window, letting the rain and leaves and everything unwanted into the house.

"Ava!" Nonna called out. But it was too late.

33

"Hazel! Red!" Ava was running as fast as she could, scanning the trees. "Come back. I need you to help me!"

Branches swung wildly in the rain. "Please come back!" She had found herself slipping down the back side of the property, where the rainwater was collecting into large pools wherever the ground dipped.

She came to the edge of the island and looked out onto the bay. Newly formed streams were flowing down the rocks and into the lake below. "Hazel!" Ava shouted out across the lake. "Red! You have to help me!"

The mainland stared back at her. Ava couldn't believe what she saw. Trees were downed along the shore, and stormwater was flooding the new road, flowing over everything, cascading off the rocks, and pulling whatever it could into the lake. Part of the parking lot had collapsed, staining the lake a reddish brown. The churned-up water stretched as far as her grandparents' island, leading Ava's eye directly downward.

The Beast lay there, capsized against the rocks, hidden under the trees.

"Cody!" Ava screamed, running panicked along the cliff edge until she found a path down the steep rocks. Though Cody MacDonald was nowhere to be seen, there was evidence of him everywhere: the tackle box he kept worms in, his fishing rod, a life jacket floating between the smooth boulders.

But Ava knew where to find him. The water was up to her chest by the time she managed her way to the boat. She knew he was there. She waded waist-deep through the murky water, which was up to her chest by the time she managed to reach the boat. The sparkly red stripe of the Beast was now dull and scratched. That dreadful feeling inside kept pulling her along, reminding her of Cody's number one rule of having a boat: a captain always stays with his ship.

34

"Cody MacDonald, I know you're under there!" Ava yelled, knocking on the underside of Cody's boat. "Come on out!"

A gale wind came through the bay, and Ava felt the boat shift and swing. The rocks were slippery beneath her feet. She took a deep breath and ducked under the water, coming up inside the overturned boat.

"Ava!" Cody exclaimed in the darkness.

"Cody, what are you doing? We've got to get out of here!"

"Perfect timing," he grunted. "We got to kick the Beast to shore! It's stuck on this big rock. You have to help me!"

Ava's eyes were still adjusting to the darkness. She could make out Cody pushing on the roof of the boat, trying to lift it.

"Are you crazy? Just forget about it! It's just a stupid boat!"

"It's not stupid!" he shouted, repositioning himself on the boulder and lifting. "It's my boat!" The hull came down with a violent scrape. "We can move it, Ava. See that boulder underwater? You got to come and stand on it. I swear, the two of us can save the Beast."

He wasn't making any sense, but Ava understood what it meant to want to save something you love, even if it was impossible to save. "Fine," she said, moving next to him. "Shift over." They began to push, and the hull came free of the boulder.

"See!" Cody strained. "We're doing it!" The boat fell back into the water and immediately turned and drifted. Ava's feet slipped from under her. She grabbed hold of the bench that went across the whole frame of the boat, and they hung on, like the two of them were on the monkey bars together.

"That's it!" Cody cried, out of breath. "Now we just have to kick it ashore."

But Ava was already kicking with all her strength. There was no controlling the boat against all that wind, and Ava knew then they were starting to drift out into the lake. The rain beat down louder as they slipped out from under the trees.

"We've got to swim for it, Cody," Ava pleaded with him. "We can't save the Beast."

"No!" Cody shouted. "The Beast can't sink. It can't!"

Ava could hear his anger and the frantic kicking of his feet. "Cody, we're drifting out into the lake!" she said, but Cody MacDonald wouldn't answer her. He just kept kicking. It was useless to argue with him. The boat tipped heavily to one side, and they had to work to keep it balanced. Ava wanted to swim away. She didn't want to be beneath a boat when it went under.

Last summer, her father had taught her what to do if her canoe flipped over. They had spent a whole morning in the shallows, her father showing her how to swim out from under it so she wouldn't bump her head or get trapped underneath.

He practiced tipping the canoe on her, repeatedly, until swimming safely away was something she did naturally and without thinking. The thing that stuck with her most is that they could never turn the canoe back over once it flipped. They always had to drag it back into the shallows. Out in deeper water, it was only a matter of time before it sank.

"Cody, we have to swim." Ava was trying to talk calmly, trying to find a way to reason with him. "We've got to get out from under here. Do you understand me?"

Cody stopped kicking, but Ava couldn't see him well enough in the darkness to know what he was thinking.

"No," he finally said to her. The firmness in his voice was gone, and what was left sounded cold and withdrawn.

Ava wanted to tell him that she understood. He was going to lose his boat, and there was nothing they could do about it. Once they swam back to shore, Ava promised herself that she would tell Cody how she lost Hazel and Red, just like he had lost his boat. She would tell him how her mother was in surgery and there was nothing she could do to help her.

They would walk back to the cabin and call his father to tell him that Cody was safe. They could ride out the rest of the storm together, just sitting there watching the rain, waiting to hear news about her mother and what the curse would do to her family, waiting and hoping that everything would be fine.

The water rose around Ava's shoulders. There was less and less space to breathe. Cody must have noticed it too. The water slipped up to their necks.

"It's sinking, Cody. We've got to swim for it."

She took deep breaths, gathering her strength to swim, waiting for Cody MacDonald to admit to himself that there was no saving the Beast.

"No," Cody answered quietly. "Ava, listen . . ."

The clouds rumbled, reminding them they had no business being out there in that water. That they should be anywhere else but in that lake.

"I can't swim."

35

"What do you mean you can't swim!" Ava screamed. She reached for him in the darkness, feeling his bare shoulders. "You're not even wearing a life jacket!"

"I forgot, okay?" Cody said quietly.

Ava felt a panic come over her. She searched around the sides of the boat for a buoy, but everything seemed to have fallen out and the hull was empty. "Come on," he said. She could hear his hands fumbling, clutching the sides of the hull. "The back of the boat is flatter. I can climb out and pull myself up."

Ava felt him slip away from her and dunk underwater. She dove clear under the boat and came up into the storm and rain. Cody had already managed to climb up onto the overturned boat. Lying flat on his stomach, he dragged himself up toward the propeller.

"Help me with this clamp," he groaned, but he was already pulling the outboard loose. The clamp fell away, and the motor dropped into the lake.

The Beast floated higher out of the water, lighter without the weight of the engine and connecting gas tank.

Cody MacDonald lay there on top of the Beast, the rain coming down all around them. He sat up and drew his knees to his chest and tried to smile at Ava, but Ava could see the fear in his eyes; he too was taking in just how far they had drifted. They were closer to the open lake than the shore, and nowhere near her grandparents' island.

Ava looked around for the shortest distance to land. Deer Island was barely visible in all that rain. "I'll go for help," she said, swimming away.

"No!" Cody cried after her. "Don't go. What if . . . what if I need you?"

Ava swam back to him, unsure of what she would do if the Beast sank. She looked around for help, but the cabins along the shore were lost in the fog. Ava squinted as the rain jumped from the surface of the lake.

"You should grab on to the boat." Cody shivered.

"I'm okay," Ava answered, treading an eggbeater. She was sure the boat would sink if she dared put her weight on it. "I can do this forever." She wasn't lying to him. She was the strongest swimmer in her swim team for three years counting, and that included the boys' team. There were some boys who were bigger, but bigger didn't mean everything if your timing is all off.

Ava looked at Cody MacDonald differently then. She studied the thickness of his legs and the width of his shoulders. He was clearly heavier than she was, and she knew that she would never be able to carry him in the water. She'd seen the older kids in swim class taking their lifeguard test, and there was always one part that terrified her. It was when you carry a classmate on your chest and swim from one end of the pool to the other. Ava had tried to carry Ruby once, just in the shallow end, and she didn't make it more than a few strokes before she was stuck on the bottom.

As the wind and rain picked up, the front of the boat dipped under the surface of the lake. Ava screamed but

Cody scrambled to hold on. Half-submerged, he grabbed on to the back of the boat, which only a moment ago held the engine. "It's sinking," he cried, his eyes closed.

"You're fine," Ava said, swimming right next to him, feeling the furthest away from fine she'd ever felt in her life. "See. It stopped."

It was true. The boat had stopped sinking and tilted back upward. The back end was bobbing there in the water, holding Cody MacDonald, while the nose of the boat pointed downward into the darkness of the lake.

"I'll teach you how to float on your back," Ava said to him. "Just in case."

Cody had yet to open his eyes.

"You know, I taught my best friend how to float last summer in less than a minute. The whole trick is to relax . . . That's all there is to it. You just relax and fall backward . . . You just stretch out like a starfish . . . but whatever you do, don't try and swim or grab on, okay? You've just got to relax, and you'll float. Got it? . . . Got it, Cody?"

"I can't do it," Cody said, shivering.

"You've just got to relax. That's the secret . . . From

now on you're not Cody MacDonald. You're a starfish. Okay . . . Say it. Say you're a starfish. Say it, Cody."

"I'm a starfish," Cody moaned.

"Good," Ava managed to say, feeling her own muscles tense and her breaths getting shorter. She was tiring too fast. She stopped talking then. She tried to slow her breathing and focus her kicks, saving her energy for the big swim she knew was just ahead.

She worried how much longer they would have to wait before someone might spot them. Hidden in all that fog and rain, they were impossible for anyone to see. One bright life jacket and they'd have been fine, Ava thought. *A life jacket would have changed everything. We'd be safe.*

Cody can't swim.

Ava kept looking around for help. Deer Island now and again poked through the fog. It cleared for a moment, long enough that Ava saw a herd of deer huddled beneath the birches. They were staring back at her and Cody, their eyes wide.

Lightning flashed, turning the lake silver, and in that sudden flash of light, Ava swore she recognized the fawn with its mother, no longer small or spotted like she'd first seen, but instead a tinier version of the adult deer around it. For some reason she half expected that fawn to recognize her—to enter the water and help her. But of course, the fawn didn't do anything at all.

The boat tilted, and Cody grabbed at Ava with his one free arm, trying desperately to keep his balance. The weight of him came down on Ava's shoulder. She kicked back with all her strength, surprised that she was able to hold him steady and keep treading water without being pushed under.

Cody screamed.

"You're fine," Ava gasped, straining to focus on the movement of her arms and the alternating pattern of her feet. "You've just got to stay like this. Look. The boat is higher."

Even Cody must have seen this was true. With only half of his weight on the boat, the hull came up again out of the water.

"Here," Ava told him. "Put your arm like this . . . on my shoulder." Ava placed Cody's hand, as if teaching him to dance. He was leaning so close to Ava that she could feel his breath on her skin. The boat steadied.

"See?" she told him between breaths. "Half your weight is on me now . . . We've just got to stay like this and everything's going to be fine . . . Just remember you're a starfish. Okay? . . . Cody, say you're a starfish."

"I'm a starfish," Cody whimpered. Ava nodded and gave a weak smile. She could hear her own heavy breath, feel her tiredness in her chest. They were nose to nose, looking at each other. His arm had slipped until it was completely around her shoulders. Ava felt all this, but there was no moving away.

"You're a starfish," she said again, finding it a comfort not just to Cody but to herself. To Ava, the words somehow meant that everyone Ava loved was in that water alongside her, and together they were all trying to float above whatever was trying to sink them—whatever current was determined to take them under.

Somewhere out in all that fog was the grave of the woodpecker. She turned her head in the direction of the island.

"I take it back . . ." she whispered. "I'm sorry for everything I said. I didn't have a right to say it. I take back every word."

Cody shook his head. "You don't have to apologize to

me," he answered. "It's all my fault . . . I'm the one that got you into this mess . . . I'm the one that's sorry."

Ava looked back at Cody MacDonald, not wanting to correct him. They waited there in the water in silence, Ava half expecting some sign from the lake to answer her, for the sky to rumble or lightning to strike them, for the curse to come to its end and for whatever was to happen to finally happen. But somehow they stayed miraculously where they were.

If anything, she noticed that the storm had let up, and the windswept lake was no longer whitecapped. The boat lifted and the rain was no more than a drizzle.

"Hear that?" Cody said, looking around. There was a hum of a motorboat somewhere in the distance. "That's my dad's boat! I'd recognize that sound anywhere!"

Ava couldn't help but grow just as excited. They searched the thinning fog as the hum of the boat grew louder. "It's him!" Cody exclaimed, craning his neck. "Hey! Over here!"

Ava tried to rise up to get a better look around the lake, but Cody was leaning too hard on her shoulder, driving her underwater.

"Don't!" Ava gasped, kicking back up, but it was too late. Cody must have realized he was pushing Ava under, because he shifted at once, setting all his weight onto the Beast.

In one swift motion, the boat sank, sending him toppling backward into the water.

"Cody!" Ava screamed, reaching for him, but it all happened in an instant. Before Ava could grab hold of his hand, Cody MacDonald was gone.

36

Ava took a deep breath and dove, swimming and reaching for Cody, watching the boat sink away into the darkness beneath him. Underwater, Cody was the opposite of a starfish. He was wild with fear, flailing and grabbing at her, until his legs wrapped around her waist.

The horrible feeling of being pulled under made Ava push violently away. She put her knee against his stomach and kicked herself free.

Every cold swim class came rushing back to her then, the dozens of certificates that hung in her room, the endless parade of after-school swim meets, the long summer days all alone in her pool swimming out of pure boredom, the months of diving again and again after the colored rings that she had tossed into the deep end. In those fleeting seconds, it all returned. She suddenly felt that moving about the water was more natural to her than anything else in the world.

She swam behind Cody and grabbed under his armpits, then towed him upward, her legs and shoulders burning with pain. He was slipping from her hands, but she managed with the very last of her strength to lift him until, at last, their heads were above water. She was trying to swim on her back while he lay across her stomach, but his heaviness was too much and kept pulling them both under.

"Cody!" she cried, but Cody MacDonald's eyes were closed. It didn't look to her like he was breathing. She felt that pulling feeling, the one she'd felt all summer, come back stronger than ever. But this time it didn't feel like a current taking Ava away but something pulling her close to Cody, calling for her to do anything to save him.

Ava took hold of Cody's head and locked her lips to his. She pinched his nose and blew into his mouth, just like she had seen the teenagers do in swim class, bending over the CPR dummy, hoping that some air from her lungs could somehow make its way to him.

And in that briefest moment, Cody MacDonald's chest expanded just enough that he opened his eyes. His arms spread outward as the two of them sank back down into the water, Ava's lips still sealed to his. This time Cody didn't struggle underwater, but stared back at Ava with a surprised look on his face, as Ava gave him the very last of her breath.

And all at once Ava realized they were not alone. Two shadowy shapes came plunging into the water, pulling Cody MacDonald away from her and grabbing at her waist, taking a firm hold of her shoulders and hauling her out of the lake, until she could feel the air burning as it rushed back into her lungs.

She didn't know where she was, only that somehow she was saved. Ava looked up, bleary-eyed and stunned like a caught fish gasping for air, desperate to know if Cody MacDonald the starfish had been hauled up alongside her.

37

"Everyone's okay," Nonno said. Her grandparents were looking down at her, waiting for Ava to respond, but Ava was unable to speak. Her chest was heaving. She lay on the deck of Mr. MacDonald's boat in a daze. Her grandmother's hand pressed up against her face. "You're all right, bella," she said over and over. "Everyone's all right. Ava, we were looking all over for you! Thank goodness we found you."

Cody lay next to her in his father's arms. "Cody, say something if you can," Mr. MacDonald begged. Cody turned to one side, coughing hard. Ava was relieved to see him sit up onto his elbows. He wiped the hair from his eyes and looked over to Ava. She couldn't understand his expression. For some reason, she thought, he had the strangest, dopiest look on his face.

"C-P-R," he said, smiling bigger than she'd ever seen. "I need CPR."

"Oh please," Ava answered, unable to see how he had missed the part where she had tried to save his life.

"Here, put these on," Nonna said, handing them both life jackets. "I can't stand another second of seeing you two without one. And CPR is serious, Cody MacDonald, especially out in the water. We can thank our lucky stars you didn't need it."

Ava shared a look with Cody, and her stomach went empty, like the moment going down a roller coaster when you can't breathe. It hit her then, as she was sure it came to Cody, how lucky they both were to be alive. They had gotten away with something dangerous, something she should have never tried in a million years. It frightened her to admit it, almost as much as it frightened her to admit to herself that she had basically gone and kissed Cody MacDonald.

"Son, you sure can pick the worst mornings to go fishing," Mr. MacDonald said.

Cody's face went sour. "I lost it, Dad. I lost the Beast."

"Oh, Cody," his father said, hugging him. "It was just a boat."

Nonna couldn't stop kissing Ava on top of her head. "Ava, that was a very brave thing helping Cody like you did. Your parents would be so proud."

Ava looked up at her grandmother, too afraid to ask what she wanted to ask.

"B-but I'm not brave at all," she stammered. "I've never been brave. Not to them. I should have been thinking about them all this time. But now it's too late. Now my mother . . . and my brothers."

Nonna stared back at Ava, blinking. "Whatever you're going on about, young lady, your mother is just fine. Everyone is fine. We called your father from the marina. That's where we thought you had run off to in the first place—to call them yourself. Anyway, you have two very healthy baby brothers. We'll go to visit them as soon as we can."

Ava looked over to Cody with surprise. He smiled back at her. "I do?" Ava said. "And they're okay?"

"They're just fine." Nonna laughed. "And look at me, young lady. When I say you're brave, you're brave. End of story. Got it?" She kissed Ava hard on the cheek. "My granddaughter, the fish."

Ava wiped her eyes, unable to stop smiling at her grandmother. The motor started up, and Mr. MacDonald drove at a slow crawl. The storm was over, and the lake was strangely calm. The morning sun broke through the pines, sweeping across the treetops and shining brightly on Deer Island. They all watched quietly as one by one the deer came out from under the trees. Together, they began grazing on the island grass, side by side, paying little attention to Mr. MacDonald's boat as it passed.

"Would you look at that," Nonna said softly. "It's like every deer in the lake country has gathered here."

Mr. MacDonald kept the boat close enough to shore that Ava saw the many birds appearing in the branches of the trees, fluffing themselves and shaking the wetness from their feathers. They were gathering close together, calling brightly back and forth, congregated in greater and greater numbers.

"I hope Hazel and Red are safe," Ava said to Nonna.

"Oh, I'm sure they're somewhere around here," Nonna answered, leaning her head on Ava's.

Mr. MacDonald weaved the boat around all the debris left behind by the storm. Nonno fished out a piece of dock wood and placed it across the front of the bow. Every cottage they passed was badly damaged, some worse than others. "We should have a look around to see if anyone needs any help," Mr. MacDonald said, turning the boat until they hugged the shore.

Ava recognized every cabin. An old hemlock had come down on the roof of the blue boat house, its pale green branches jutting right out of the broken windows. A sailboat had capsized in the marina, and several parked cars were damaged by fallen branches and trees.

There was no booming sound coming from the building of the new road. Along with the songbirds came the voices of the cottagers around the bay. People were out again, checking in on one another, fishing out docks that had broken away, and rescuing what they could from the lake. Generators hummed to life and saws began to work, cutting away at the downed trees.

Behind her grandparents' island, the low-lying section

of the new road was flooded. The storm had split the construction parking lot in half, eroding the shore. The massive dump trucks and an excavator—machines that once looked indestructible to Ava—were either sunk into the mud or tipped over.

"It doesn't look like they'll make much progress on the road for a while," Nonno said.

The morning air turned cool, and the clouds had thinned and brightened into wisps of light. When Mr. MacDonald pulled up to her grandparents' cabin, they saw the dock splintered against the rocks and every bit of the garden flattened, plowed over by the wind. The screen porch had been torn open, and an elm had come down, shattering the porch railing and blocking the pathway to the stairs.

"Oh no," Ava said. "It's all destroyed."

Nonno climbed down from the boat and into the shallow water. "Nothing ruined we can't fix or that won't grow again."

There was a cheerful trill from the trees, a song that Ava immediately recognized. "Hazel! Red!" Ava cried, though her voice was no more than a whisper. She waved to the two birds but fought the urge to call out for them again. The robins took off high into the air, circling and singing for a moment before flying off into the distance.

Ava sat back in the boat and looked at Cody MacDonald, trying to swallow the disappointment.

"It sucks, I know," Cody said to her, defeated. "We lost everything. Hazel and Red, the Beast, my best fishing rod. What are we going to do now?"

"Well, Cody, it's still another couple of weeks before school starts," Mr. MacDonald said. "I'll phone your mother and see about us staying longer and lending folks a hand. We could call this place home for a little longer. What do you think, Ava? Sound like a fair deal?"

Cody and Ava smiled at each other.

"It's a deal," Ava said.

38

It was the last week of August, and the lake was alive with people preparing for the colder season ahead. Boats were being pulled from the lake, and barges of supplies were heading to repair the island cabins affected by the storm. The weather was pleasant; like the mosquitos, the summer heat seemed to have vanished overnight after the storm.

Ava stayed too, helping her grandparents. Without the responsibility of taking care of Hazel and Red, there was plenty of time in the day. She even went fishing with Cody MacDonald, though she never once caught anything or saw a pike. She had marked the twenty-eighth of the month on the fridge calendar, and on that day, she got a call from the marina that sent her bursting out of the front porch of the cabin.

"They're here!" she shouted, running barefoot down to the dock. "They're here!"

"Nonno's been ready all morning," her grandmother said from the garden. "I'll be waiting right here for you all. There's not enough room on that boat to hold all of us."

Ava's grandfather was seated at the bow of the boat. Ava had seen him pretending to read the same page of the newspaper, hiding his excitement. "You drive," he said to her.

"Okay," Ava said, hopping into the back. He had switched out the larger motor with an old eight-horsepower engine, low-powered enough that Ava was permitted to drive. The old motor had a pull start, and Ava yanked on it until a wheel spun on top and the engine got going.

Ava made a straight line for the marina, knowing that Cody MacDonald would recognize the sound of her boat, and from halfway across the bay she spotted him waving from the water. He had on a life jacket and was doggie-paddling around his dock, showing off as always whenever Ava gave him the time of day.

"Nice moves!" she called to him. Cody climbed up onto his dock and put his hands to his lips, blowing kiss after kiss to her.

"Get over it already," Ava said to herself, shaking her head.

She steered her way between the boats racing in and out of the marina, guiding them toward the open dock where her parents were waiting for her. Ava noticed them even at a distance. They were standing under the shaded rooftop that kept the marina's single gas pump out of the sun.

Ava cut the engine and drifted in, all the while her eyes set on the two baby boys in her parents' arms. They were wrapped in blue blankets, like two robin's eggs.

"They look like Hazel and Red," Ava said to her grandfather.

"They do?" Nonno laughed, grabbing ahold of the dock. He wrapped the rope around the mooring. "Maybe so."

"Ava!" her mother called as her father waved her over. "Come here and meet your brothers." But Ava had already leapt from the boat, smiling as the solid dock under her feet led her home.

Acknowledgments

When I was eleven years old, my parents decided on a small cabin in the Kawartha Lakes region of Ontario, Canada. That is where I spent my summers, and I have my parents to thank for that experience in nature, which shaped not only who I am, but what type of artist I would later find out I wanted to be.

Grazie mille and 감사합니다 to both sides of my family, as well as the dear friends who were early readers of this story and gave their time, thoughts, and support so generously.

Also, I owe an enormous debt to Karen Lotz, Ann Stott, Lydia Abel, Jackie Houton, Julia Gaviria, Gregg Hammerquist, Erin Farley, Tracy Miracle, Laura Rivas, Alice McConnell and Kim Smith, and Janine Kamouh and Aimee Greenebaum. There simply wouldn't be a novel without them.